Twitter: @LEckhart
Facebook: AuthorLorhainneEckhart

Printed in the U.S.A

THRILL OF THE CHASE

The Parker Sisters

LORHAINNE ECKHART

"Two people who couldn't be more different find themselves thrown together in a life or death situation."

Susan, Reviewer

"Seriously cannot get enough of Lorhainne Eckhart's books! She's my favorite author and truly amazing!"

Lori Reviewer

"What happens with an overprotective family and a buddy romance?"

Irish eyes

He stopped for an accident and stumbled upon the one woman he'd been looking for all his life.

From a Readers' Favorite award-winning author and the "queen of the family saga" (Aherman) comes The Parker Sisters, a new spinoff of the Married in Montana series.

To everyone who doesn't know her, dependable EMT Taz Parker is strong, capable, and confident. However, everything about her job terrifies her. She lives in a small Wyoming town, with four sisters, an overprotective father, and no dating prospects on the horizon, considering the lack of available men in the area. That is until one rainy night, while transporting a patient to the next town, she stumbles upon an accident.

Jerry O'Rourke is only passing through town when he witnesses a roadside accident. When he stops to help at the grisly scene, there's only so much he can do, so he flags down a passing ambulance. A pretty EMT stops to help, and Jerry is unable to resist her.

Even though he lives in another state, Jerry seeks out Taz just one more time—but what he encounters is a naive young woman from a big family. Taz is beautiful and innocent, and he wonders where she's been all his life. When he sets his sights on her, he soon realizes that the strong ties Taz has with her family could make having her far more difficult than he could have ever imagined.

T az wanted a hot bath, a good book, and a slice of Hoover's Meat Lover's Paradise, the specialty pizza at the Dog House. In fact, she could see herself wrapped in her fluffy lavender robe, wool socks on her feet, curled up on the sofa, digging into that first slice, which would comfort her after a lousy day at the station. Her workplace was a run-down double wide, all the town of Kaycee could provide for its EMTs, and her arrogant partner from Buffalo was four years her junior.

Today, she had rushed to a scene only to be turned away by a chauvinistic good ol' boy who'd rather have died than be rescued by a woman. Taz hadn't minded the fact that the idiot saw her as a member of the weaker sex or the fact that he'd insisted Bradley Dunlop, a.k.a. her arrogant partner, who was still in training, be the one to administer first aid. It hadn't been a big deal, even considering the man had had a hatchet sticking out of his back. How he'd managed that feat, she hadn't a clue.

Even though Bradley looked about twelve and weighed

only one twenty, the balding overweight man had insisted he was his guy because, being male, he'd know more about what he was doing. That was laughable, considering Bradley still had to be reminded of some pretty basic rules —for example, that when he stepped out of the ambulance after getting the call, he needed to assess the scene and take a few commonsense steps. Look left, look right, and don't forget to look up.

She could hear the victim caterwauling and listened to the back and forth as she stood five steps away, that is, after she'd cut down the smoldering tree branch the guy had been sitting under. If Bradley had only looked up and assessed the scene as he was supposed to have done, he'd have seen it was only moments away from falling onto the shirtless idiot, whose fat belly was sticking out over his ripped blue jeans. She took in what she supposed was the barn, or rather a shed with rotted boards, a door hanging from one hinge, and rusty farm implements and piles of black garbage bags scattered everywhere, obviously the source of the rank odor that had hit her as she first stepped out of the rig.

"So how, again, did you get an ax in your back?" Bradley asked. He was on the ground, squatting, wrapping the gushing wound. Blood was pooling on the gauze, and the man was glassy eyed. Taz had to bite her tongue, fighting the urge to correct Bradley. It was a hatchet, not an ax. Big difference.

"I tripped. Goddamn fool woman didn't put the thing back, and next thing I knew, I had this blade jammed in my back."

Taz took in Wilma, the wife of the idiot on the ground, who was also standing five feet back. She wasn't a looker and appeared to be in her fifties, with salt and pepper hair that seemed to give her a bad hair day every day. She was wearing a faded house dress with an apron overtop, her face overly wrinkled, her eyes tired. She crossed her bony arms across her skinny chest. Her lips were thin, and she was shaking her head.

"Hap, you were weaving out here, dragging that thing and throwing it around, drunker than a skunk—"

"Oh, you hush up there, woman," Hap snapped.

Taz couldn't figure out why Wilma had stuck around, not that she knew these folks well. They had four grown boys, one doing a nickel of hard time for holding up a liquor store, another having enlisted in the army and been shipped off to some godforsaken country overseas, and the other two having fucked off somewhere. They had obviously been smart enough to realize that sticking around here with parents who took dysfunctional to a whole new level would get them a life in prison, living hand to mouth, or, if they were really lucky, following in their parents' footsteps.

Taz hoped they'd found a better life as she watched Wilma pull a cigarette and lighter with a shaky hand from a torn pocket of her apron. She slipped it into her mouth, lit it, and took a heavy drag. Taz could hear her lungs scraping, and then she coughed deep and long, waving her hand at Taz when she started toward her. It was always the same with Wilma: the cigarettes, the coughing, the wheezing—and then there was the booze. Wilma just hid it better, but Taz could smell the cheap gin from fifteen feet away.

"Bradley…" Taz said and gestured with her chin to the spilled beer off to one side and what looked like dozens of empties tossed everywhere. "How much you had to drink there, Hap?" she added, wondering how people could live the way they lived.

"I ain't going to tell you again there, missy. You let this

young feller handle things and learn your place. Ouch, be careful!" the man shouted when Bradley bumped the head of the blade. Served him right, she wanted to say, and she was about to say something to Bradley when he stood up, gloves covered in blood, and stepped over to her.

"You think you could give me a hand securing that ax and then loading this guy up?" he snapped, always an asshole, acting as if he were the one who had been wronged.

"Why? What was it Hap said? I'm just a girl. You're the expert. Pretty sure by your laugh that you agreed with him," Taz said. She could hear the feline growl in her head. It wasn't often she stooped to this bitchy level. She ground her teeth, feeling the pinch in her jaw. "You seen the beer cans, the mess. Guarantee by that glassy-eyed look he's at least three times over the legal limit."

Bradley said nothing as he stared at her. It was two, three seconds before he turned his head and took in the scene, the one he was supposed to have assessed before stepping from the rig. She knew he'd missed it, considering taking direction from her didn't sit that well with him. He was young and thought he knew everything, just another asshole who fit in with what seemed to be a way of life out here.

He said nothing as he looked back to her, taking on the pissed-off expression that shouldn't have bothered her as much as it did. Heavy clouds had started drifting in shortly after they'd pulled in, and the wind was whipping up. The temperature was dropping, too, and she expected rain to spit from the sky any second.

"Hmm," Bradley said and then gave her his back, walking over to Hap just as the first drop of rain hit the ground. "Grab the stretcher, bring it on out here, and let's load him up," he ordered, obviously accepting the promotion Hap had bestowed. In Taz's mind, this put Bradley somewhere between a shithead and a dung beetle.

Wilma gave her a pathetic look that seemed to say, "Come on, girl. Hurry the fuck up." Then she lifted her hand to keep the gathering rain from soaking the cigarette still dangling from her lips, an inch of ash ready to fall.

With Hap now loaded in the back, Taz was behind the wheel, leaving Bradley with his newfound friend for the trek to Buffalo, where they would dump this idiot in the ER and get him off their—correction, her hands. She'd done the drive in thirty minutes before, but with the rain now pelting down in buckets, dropping visibility to piss poor, she'd have to tack on at least another ten as she kept the speed to something manageable. Even though the highway was flat and the traffic light, with the sun gone and the heavy clouds, the visibility was about as bad as it could be.

Then she saw something just ahead as she approached a sharp hairpin turn. There in the blind spot in a thick of trees was a car, hazards flashing. Someone was on the side of the road, waving. She gripped the wheel as she pressed the brakes, feeling the water under the wheels just as she rounded the bend. She thought it was a man waving his arms. One car was silver, small, and another was upside down in the ditch, smoke rising. The man waving his arms ran toward the rig. She pressed the brakes harder, slowing to a stop.

"Why are you stopping?" Bradley poked his head into the front.

"Looks like an accident," she said as she pulled in behind the car, turning her flashing lights on.

"Just radio it in," he said. "We're already full up, and Hap needs to get to the ER now."

"I will call it in, and Hap will see a doctor, but I'm

stopping," she said as she put the rig in park. Then she stepped out, looking up to see that the man was tall, gorgeous, and dripping wet. He ran his hands over his head, sweeping back his dark hair, water running down his face. Taz was already soaked from the two steps it had taken to reach him.

"What happened here?" she asked.

The man was nicely dressed, his shirt soaked through and sticking to his impressive chest, and his tailored pants appeared expensive, designer, name brand. His shirt sleeves were rolled up, with blood on his cuffs.

"Drove up on an accident," he said. "One guy's stuck, one pinned underneath—dead, I think. I just called it in."

"Taz, leave it. Let's go," Bradley called out and actually honked the horn, sounding much like a two-year-old instead of a guy who was supposed to help others. He hadn't even bothered to step out.

She had no patience to deal with idiots any more today, so she ignored him as she took a second to assess the over-turned car. The man looked back to the rig, most likely looking for the idiot who wouldn't get out and help. There was water on the road, still poor visibility, and she saw what she thought was smoke or maybe steam rising from the crash site.

Then the guy touched her arm and said, "Come on. I need some help." As she started behind the guy, sliding into the ditch, he grabbed her arm. "Watch your footing," he said. "It's slippery."

She heard tires squeal as her ambulance, the one she was responsible for, pulled away.

"Bradley, you fucking idiot!" she yelled out. Then, when she hit a patch of mud, she lost her footing and tumbled down, hitting the good Samaritan and knocking his feet from under him. They both tumbled down the embankment, and he landed right on top of her.

Chapter Two

It was a horrible scene, and one Jerry O'Rourke thought he'd never clear from his mind. The dead guy was pinned under the rundown import, its rear wheel still spinning. Everything about the situation was surreal, including the fact that he was now on the ground on top of the paramedic with dark hair and deep blue eyes. She had landed face first in the mud, and he pushed off her back and then slipped onto his ass. The once attractive lady lifted her face, gasping for air.

"I told you to watch your step," Jerry said. He couldn't believe any of this was really happening, especially that the ambulance was now speeding away. What kind of place was this? He was on his feet now, wiping the mud from his hands and his ruined Alfred Sung pants. His dress shoes too would need a heavy cleaning, as he could feel the wet muck squishing between his toes.

The paramedic was on her knees, wiping the mud from her face, which only smeared it more. Then she slid down the rest of the way to the car and squatted down. "You call for help?" she asked without looking back as she reached in. Then she said something to the guy hanging upside down, still belted in.

Jerry made his way down the bank and leaned over her, the rain still coming down in sheets. He was past feeling the chill, which had penetrated skin deep. He needed a towel—or better, a hot shower and coffee. Still, he wondered if even that would warm him. His suit jacket was in the backseat, but he wasn't interested in ruining that as well. Was he going to have to call 911 again?

"I called it in just before you got here," he said. "That's why you're here, right? So why did your partner take off, seriously?" He still couldn't believe the sight of the guy yelling out the window as he climbed behind the wheel of the ambulance before flicking on the siren, lights still flashing, and speeding away. Jerry couldn't hear the siren anymore now.

"Not us," she said. "We were coming from another scene and had a guy in back who needed to get to a hospital."

Then he caught it: The sound, although faint, was a siren in the distance. "That must be them, then. How is he?"

The guy in the car was quiet now. Before, he had been carrying on, his arms hanging, blood dripping. The paramedic pressed her fingers to his neck. She was concentrating through the mud and the rain that was washing it away in streaks, her hair dripping over the collar of her blue coat. "Weak pulse," she said. "Sir, can you hear me? Can you tell me where it hurts?" When the guy moaned and said nothing, she leaned in and looked around. "You said there was someone else?"

Yeah, there had been, and Jerry wasn't too keen to recall the image. "Other side, pinned under, not moving. Pretty sure he's dead."

It was the unseeing eyes, the way they looked up at the sky and there was nothing in them—the stillness, the fact he hadn't been able to find a pulse. Creepy and unsettling.

She tapped the car as she went to stand and moved around the other side. He followed, hearing the sirens coming closer. He should go up to the road, but he also didn't want to leave this lady even though he was pretty sure she may have seen and handled worse.

Her hands were on the man's face, and she closed his eyes. She was squatting down beside him. His body below the shoulders was pinned underneath the car. "You're right," she said. "Dead, probably thrown." She was looking into the car, bending over at the waist. "Not wearing a seatbelt, from the looks of things. Stupid idiot," she muttered.

He could see the lights coming now, the blare of the siren louder. Just as she leaned in the vehicle again, there was a grinding sound of metal that had him reaching for her hips, pulling her back as the car slid. He linked his arms around her waist and lifted her, taking a giant step and moving her out of the way, his feet sliding in the mud. He landed with her on the ground just as there was another crash and bang. The car had slid into a boulder, and here he was with this young woman, his arms linked around her waist, holding her on the ground as the rain pelted down. The ambulance and rescue vehicle pulled up. A rock was jabbing into his hip.

"Well, you can let go of me now," the woman snapped, pushing against his groin with her soft rounded ass as she got onto her knees. Whatever zinged between them in that moment was electric, but the look on her face was furious as she stared at him and wiped her hair back. Then she lifted her hand toward the arriving ambulance.

"Got one pinned in the car!" she said. "Need help getting him out."

She was still talking as she made her way back up the hill, and he rolled to his side in the mud, the rain hitting his face as he squinted and looked up in the dark at the lights, the emergency vehicles and workers making their way down the hill.

He had thought it was a good idea to drive home from Billings to Denver after a meeting with a firm he was interested in buying as an addition to O'Rourke Security. The drive should have been relaxing, giving him the time he needed to plan out his next steps, but instead he'd almost been run off the road as those good ol' boys blew past him. They had tossed a beer can out the window, tunes cranked, before losing control and flipping twice, then landing in the ditch. And here Jerry was in the middle of nowhere, freezing, soaked, muddy, and angry. One of the men was dead, and the other was barely alive, and all he could think as he sat in the mud was *What a waste.*

Chapter Three

"Taz, I know you're angry. We've heard Bradley's side too, and he may have jumped the gun, but you were both right and both wrong, so we've decided it would be best to just let things go. He was understandably concerned for the patient, who'd lost a distressing amount of blood, was in shock, and…"

Taz pulled the phone away from her ear, staring at the receiver, hearing Clarice, her boss, rattle on and on. She was pacing the floor of her small cabin, one of three her father had built for her and each of her sisters on his thirty-acre spread, which was less than fifty feet from the front door of her parents' house. Clarice headed up the emergency services for Johnson County, and she was someone who never wanted to make waves. Taz was well aware that the "we" she spoke of was most likely the Johnson family, who Bradley was related to, who sat on the council and the fire department and held office in Buffalo, where Bradley was from.

"Clarice, he left me there, pulled away. He's reckless

and has no respect for authority. And, just so we're clear, Hap's wound wasn't life threatening. Nothing major was hit, and he'd been stitched up and loaded with heavy antibiotics…" She stopped talking, as the heavy sigh coming through the phone had her feeling as if she were whining and Clarice had stopped listening. She didn't have a clue how to get her point across, how to get Clarice to back her and reprimand the idiot she was stuck with. At times, she was sure Clarice was far more interested in fitting into a man's world than doing what was right.

"You couldn't have known that for sure," she replied. "From what I understand from Bradley, the patient wasn't comfortable with you, and he was forced to step in and run the scene."

Her throat closed up. That little shit had twisted the entire situation. "That is not what happened, Clarice. That's not fair. Hap is a good ol' drunk fucker who hates women—" Again the sigh, so she stopped talking. "Fine, but from now on give Bradley to someone else. I'd just as soon work with one of the volunteer EMTs."

The volunteers were three overweight balding guys over fifty who weren't related but looked the same. They were polite, helpful, and always deferred to her, the only paid fulltime female EMT in Kaycee.

"Is this going to become an issue, Taz? Because you know that's not going to happen. Bradley's father is…"

Oh my God, here we go again. She pulled the phone away because she knew exactly how Bradley fit into the equation. He was the useless son of Buffalo's fire chief, and the Johnson family was deeply ingrained in and around Buffalo. Bradley had the attitude and work ethic of a kid who'd never had to work at figuring out what he wanted to do. Everything he did had been handed to him. "I know, Clarice. Thanks for pointing out that Johnson

County emergency services is about who you know and not your skill level. I for one will sleep a lot better at night knowing that if I were bleeding out on death's doorstep and needed emergency help, chances are I would get the loser son who can't get a job on his own and needs daddy to pull some strings. Got to say, not reassured at all that he'd put any effort into saving my life."

As soon as it was out of her mouth, she wanted to take it back. That was one of her many faults, the fact that she often spoke before thinking of the consequences. It was one her mother had pointed out time and again would get her into more hot water and trouble than she could ever imagine.

"Taz, I'm going to say this again. Nothing is going to happen, but if you keep pushing this issue, I can tell you that it will be your actions that will be scrutinized. My advice is to let it go. You won't win this one. I advised Bradley the same, considering his father has called and demanded you be written up."

Yup, totally ground into the dirt. It would be best to end this, take the night to sulk alone, and try again in the morning, when she'd had a chance to prop up her pride again. "Fine, but this isn't right, Clarice."

"Taz, pick your battles. Be smarter about your eagerness to confront authority. And, by the way, how did the guy fare from the car in the ditch?"

That was one more reason for her miserable, cranky mood. "Didn't make it," she said. He'd bled out on the way after she and the others at the scene had gotten him out of the overturned wreck. He'd been only nineteen, working at the oilfield, twice over the legal limit. The guy under the truck had been his brother. That was all she'd heard from the fellow EMT who'd shown up at the hospital accompanied by a rough redneck who was the father of the two young men.

"Sorry to hear that," Clarice said. "So we're good?"

Taz shook her head and had to force the words from her lips. "Totally," she said, and then she hung up and put the phone back in the holder.

She unbuttoned her coat, which was still damp and muddy, as she looked around her cozy cabin. The kitchen was small but efficient, the living room was quaint, with a fireplace, and her bedroom was a loft upstairs that over-looked the living area. There was a sharp knock on the door just before it opened.

No surprise that it was her mother, Susan, who was still quite beautiful, with shoulder-length salt and pepper hair and blue eyes that appeared soft and bright. It amazed her how they stood out so deceptively, making people think she was sweet and timid when she was actually tough as nails, hardworking, and strong willed. She was carrying a plate covered with a dishtowel and wearing her father's heavy denim coat. "Your father watched you pull in. You okay? You look like you crawled through the mud." She rested the plate on the small wooden table with two chairs that her father had made.

That was definitely her dad's way; he worried about all his daughters. Most likely, a wordless look from him had sent her mom over to check on her. That was her role. Taz wanted a shower and a moment, not her mom walking in and questioning her, then reporting back to her dad, who'd probably be outside, wiping out her now muddy truck. Her mother gave her a look.

"Sorry, yes, a bad scene. I fell in the mud. Just need a shower and—" She sniffed the aroma that hit her and had her mouth watering. "Is that your fried chicken?" She lifted the towel and took in the chicken with two biscuits covered in gravy, green beans, and a heap of mashed potatoes. Forget the pizza! Nothing came close to her mother's fried chicken and biscuits, and no one in this county could make gravy like her mother. She reached for the chicken, but her mother smacked her hand.

"You're a mess," Susan said. "Wash up and then you can eat. What happened tonight? I got a call from Dixie, who saw the ambulance pull out of Hap and Wilma's. You didn't go in there alone, did you?"

Of course her mother had heard, and of course she was worried. Everyone knew Hap and Wilma weren't exactly people you could be safe around. Added to that, every time there was a call around Kaycee and she responded, her mother knew the details before she even got home. Just once she'd like her family not to know something about her life, maybe have a secret or two of her own.

"Hap was drunk, as usual. Got a hatchet stuck in his back this time. You know I'm not alone. Got that newbie from Buffalo working with me." She bit her tongue before she could add how much she hated that prick. As she looked up, she took in the horror on her mother's face. She waved her hand in the air. "Hap's fine. Be home tomorrow, I'm sure."

Her mother was nodding, now rummaging in her fridge and pulling out a carton of milk Taz knew she hadn't bought. She lifted a glass from the cupboard, and Taz strode to the sink, rolled her grungy sleeves up, turned on the water, and scrubbed her hands using the dish soap. The rain and mud had soaked through everything, and she should just climb in the shower, but the chicken was calling her. She leaned down and splashed water on her face, then scrubbed to get off as much as possible of the dirt she knew was still caked there before shutting off the tap. Her mother held out a towel.

"You know, Mom, I'm a grown woman, and you coming over every night with dinner is thoughtful, but you're invading my space. And you need to stop filling my fridge with groceries."

Her mother waved her hand and rested the glass of milk on the table beside the plate, calling to her. Then she moved through Taz's kitchen, pulled open a drawer, and lifted out a napkin, a fork, and a knife to set the table as Taz dried her face and her hands. "I'm your mother, and it's what I do," Susan said. "Besides, if I left it to you, you'd starve. There was nothing in your fridge but two rotting cartons of leftover takeout, some dried cheese, and beer. Come on, sit and eat. Heard your partner left you high and dry on the side of the road, too. Heard that was a bad one."

What, was her mother psychic? She was about to ask her, and maybe it was her expression that had her mother pulling out a chair and patting it for her to sit.

"Come on, Taz. Sit, eat."

She did. Her mother sat across from her and handed her the napkin as if she'd forget, and she lifted the plump chicken thigh and took a bite. She groaned, as it tasted even better than it smelled. Some mothers were great cooks, but her mom was exceptional, taking comfort food to an entirely new level. "I would really like to be able to come home just one time without you knowing anything about my day," she said as she chewed, noting the frown on her mother's face.

"Don't talk with your mouth full," Susan said and then nothing else. Her expression was all mothering, waiting, worried. She hovered at times and butted in, always checking on her daughters.

"It was bad," Taz finally said. "Two young guys from the other side of Buffalo, drunk and joyriding, flipped in the ditch and both ended up dead."

And the good Samaritan who had stopped to help… She'd last seen him standing with one of the police officers at the scene, giving a statement, as she climbed in the back of the ambulance with the other paramedic, trying her best to keep the young man alive. She found herself wondering now who the guy was. Someone not from around here, and most likely he was long gone.

"Bradley left me at the side of the road. Nothing will happen to him, either. Just got off the phone with Clarice before you showed up. What is it, Mama, with these young useless guys who can't figure out how to stand on their own two feet? They also refuse to take direction from a woman, so they take great joy in grinding her into the dirt. I complained, and now I'm the one getting my hand slapped."

Her mother was sitting across from her and folded her hands together, shaking her head. "Taz, I've talked to you before about being smart, told you that trying to take on some white boy with connections is just plain foolish. There are times when you do something, and times when you be smarter. This is one of those times where you need to be smart and know your place. Don't you remember what I taught you? Take a minute or a day, and don't let your crazy anger show. Hold your tongue, keep it together. Don't fall apart, or cry and scream, or lose your temper and go off all half cocked, pointing figures about who's right and who's done what. Instead, you need to keep it together, and when it's really tough and you feel ground down as if it can't get any worse, don't let anyone see how they've beaten you down. Just paste a smile on your face. It sounds to me as if you just got a reaction to your anger."

Her mother lifted her hand to stop Taz when she took a breath as if to begin to set the record straight. "It's got nothing to do with you being right and them being wrong and everything to do with you knowing your place," she said. "There's nothing fair in this world, and the difference between those with everything and those with nothing is how they play the game. I'm not talking about them being better than you. It's that nobody wants to have a woman flipping out, acting all crazy and yelling and furious and righteous, even if she is right. They won't hear you. Men and especially other women will label you crazy and problematic. You want to fix the problem, you need to be the sharp one. Use your head, Taz. Be smarter, and remember men will always see you as just a pretty face first, no matter what, so use that to your advantage and calmly find a way to fix the situation your way, the right way. Then be on your way before they figure out that you just turned the tables on them."

Her mother winked and rested her hand on the table as a quiet smile touched her lips. "Finish your dinner, get in the shower, and then get some rest." She stood up and started to the door. "Oh, and I'll tell your father you'll stop in and see him in the morning. Have coffee with him before he heads out. He's picked up more work at the oilfield, machinery repair, so at least let him see for himself you're okay so he can focus on work and not worry about you." Her hand was on the door.

Taz knew what her mother was saying. Not a day went by that her father didn't worry that one of his daughters would slip away like Brandyne, their eldest sister, whom they'd lost sixteen years earlier to a rodeo cowboy just passing through. Even though they'd since reconnected with her and her new husband, living in Montana, that was a grief she never wanted to see on her parents' faces ever again.

She sighed, knowing her fate was sealed. "I will, Mama, first thing," she said, realizing she'd die here on this spread with her four sisters, single and alone. She'd never find herself a man.

Chapter Four

Jerry pulled open the door to Jimmy's Café, a diner at the edge of Kaycee with a large sign on the roof. For a small town, the place seemed crowded, and it took him a moment as he pulled his shades from his face to spot an empty stool at the counter. He'd get coffee and eggs and then hit the road. That was the plan. He smiled at a passing waitress, a short, plump older woman with a bad dye job and a wide gap between her front teeth.

"Want a table, honey?" she asked him as she lifted a menu from the stack and walked behind the counter to set it down.

"Nope, here's fine," he said.

She reached for a coffee pot and mug and set it in front of him, then started pouring before he could confirm he wanted coffee. "Cream and sugar is right here." She reached for a bowl of sweetener packages and creamer and slid those in front of him. "Just passing through?" She was chewing gum and had dimples and a spark in her eyes. Deanna was the name pinned to her pink polyester chest.

"I am, Deanna. What's good here?"

"Just about everything. The morning special is chicken fried steak with two buttermilk biscuits and Jimmy's special sausage gravy. It's spicy and has a kick, but we can tone it down if you don't like the heat." She winked, and it took him a second to realize she was flirting with him. He was stuck on the idea of the fat in that meal, thinking of the heart attack that would come with something likely floating in grease.

"How about just eggs, two, poached, with whole wheat toast?" He slid the menu to the waitress, who tsked and was staring as if he'd asked for the unthinkable.

"Sure that's all you want, honey?" She seemed disappointed, but then, he noticed a fair amount of thick bellies among the patrons in the diner.

"It's enough. Thank you kindly," he added, taking a look at the creamer, which had nothing in it, but the waitress was now gone. He spotted another container beside the lady on his right. The big guy on his left had a heavy beard and was deep into his stacked platter of flapjacks, pouring more syrup overtop. "Could you pass the cream?" he asked the woman—and then took in the startling blue eyes and the face he'd never forget. "Hey, I know you, from yesterday at the accident."

She was beautiful minus the muddy drowned rat look. She reached for the small metal pitcher and set it in front of him. Not a smile, nothing. She held her coffee, then mopped up gravy with a biscuit and chewed.

"So the gravy's good here?" he asked.

She wiped her hands and slid her plate away. "The best," she said. "That's it for me, Deanna. Can I get the bill?"

The plump waitress stopped in front of her. "Honey, told you before your money ain't any good here. It's on the house. You saving Ricky the way you did, you're a hero," she said, smiling. "Take care now. Say hello to your mama and daddy for me."

The woman stood up, pulling two bills from her pocket to set on the counter. She wore dark blue pants and a shirt, a uniform, but he couldn't help taking in her trim figure and imagining the curves hidden under it. Her hair was dark, with natural waves, just past her shoulders. She was ignoring him.

"So did he make it?" he asked, wondering about the guy in the car. Freddy, he remembered the name. The guy had pleaded with Jerry to get him out, but that had been right after the accident happened, before the paramedics had arrived, when he'd still been talking.

She stilled, and her expression was haunted when her gaze flicked to him. He wondered, by the look, what she'd seen. Her lips firmed, and she shook her head. "No, he didn't. We tried, but his injuries were far too severe. It's a waste for someone that young." She seemed to hesitate and was about to say something else, but instead she lifted her hand to the waitress. Her attention was gone again, and she gave him her back. Of course his gaze drifted to her ass. It was perfection, and he was suddenly walking right behind her and out the door. She turned startled eyes to him. "I, uh…" She was rattled.

"Listen, I never got your name, and considering the circumstances we met under, I figured it would be nice to know who you are."

She had the most expressive face he'd ever seen. "Taz," she said and held out her hand.

He took it and squeezed. It was small, soft. "Taz, pleasure to meet you. Jerry O'Rourke. Would you like to have dinner with me?"

Her mouth opened, and her breath caught as if she

was surprised or shocked. He held her hand, looking again at the ring finger. "Or am I overstepping? Is there a special someone already in your life?"

She pulled her hand away and her expression changed again, no longer rattled. "There's plenty of someones in my life." She still hadn't answered him, and he wondered for a minute whether she'd turn and leave or tell him to get lost. Maybe she was married and didn't wear a ring, or maybe she had a lover or boyfriend she spent her evenings with? Whatever it was, he couldn't pinpoint exactly where he stood.

"Dinner is all I'm asking, tonight," he said. "Unless you're seeing someone," he added again a little more forcefully. In fact, his car was packed, and he needed to get back on the road and home to Denver.

"I work until seven," she said and then nothing else. Single, taken? No idea.

"Great. Why don't I pick you up at seven and take you…" Take her where, to the diner?

A smile touched her lips, her round cheeks rosy. "How about I meet you here, say seven thirty?"

"Dinner at seven thirty. See you then, Taz," he said, and he watched as the woman he knew nothing about yet hopped into a deep green pickup and backed out. Only when she began to drive away did she turn her head to the side and look at him, and Jerry knew from that face, that look, and the energy zinging between them that there was something about this girl he had to know more about. If he explained it to anyone, they'd have said he was crazy.

Chapter Five

Her day hadn't exactly gone as planned. She'd spent one half of it in Buffalo doing paperwork and the last half playing solitaire in the rundown EMT trailer at the edge of Kaycee. She hadn't said a word to Bradley other than "Hey there," but she'd had to listen to him bouncing a small rubber ball against the wall over and over, then talking dirty with who she presumed was his girlfriend, all while she prayed for any type of call to come in and save her. Even a stubbed toe would have been welcome.

There were days when everything happened and days she was bored to tears. Those were the days she should have enjoyed, should have looked forward to, but she didn't. She loved the days she was neck deep in trauma, in an accident scene, where a split-second decision, wrong or right, would be what stood between life and death for the victim. It was those days that had her adrenaline pumping, her excitement soaring, and those days that Taz knew she was doing what she loved to do. But not today. Today had been one of the longest, most boring, most painful days in her career. To escape the dark, hateful energy she knew Bradley was shooting her way, she'd stooped to scrubbing the trailer from top to bottom, even removing the coffee stains from the burner of the pot, which had been caked on for ages.

As soon as the clock hit seven, Taz was out the door of the trailer and home to shower and change into a soft blue cowlneck sweater and new blue jeans. She added a pair of hoops, a hint of shadow, and was out the door before her mother could reach her.

"Where you off to?" Susan asked as she emerged from the house, holding another plate.

Taz could smell the meatloaf, another dish of her mother's that no one could top. "I have plans. Sorry, Mom. Smells good, though." She started down her steps, noting her mother's narrowed gaze.

"Plans with who?"

With a gorgeous guy she'd met at the side of a road in a rainstorm, trying to save the life of a young man. "Just meeting someone for dinner, is all. No one you know." She took another step, wearing the black boots with a slight heel that she'd bought on a whim a year ago but had never worn.

"Is this a guy or a girl kind of friend, because you look rather dressed up?" Her mom was still holding the towel-covered plate, her other hand on her hip, wearing faded baggy jeans and one of her older striped shirts.

Taz glanced over to the house, seeing her dad on the front porch. He'd lit his pipe, as she could see smoke. He lifted his hand to her, making her feel as if she were sixteen and needed their permission to go out. It was ridiculous. "Mom, I'm a grown woman, twenty-eight years old, and you're grilling me as if I'm a teenager. I have a job…"

"Taz Parker, how old you are doesn't make you any less

our daughter. It's called being respectful and courteous and not adding any unnecessary worry. If you're going out, we'd like to know just so we're not wondering if you're hurt somewhere or something has happened to you. I don't understand why you wouldn't want to tell me. Are you going out to the bar? If that's the case, I don't want you drinking and driving."

She wanted to roll her eyes. She should have expected this, knowing it was easier to give her mother something than to be coy. She looked at her watch: seven twenty. She needed to go.

"I'm going to the diner for dinner. You don't know them. I promise I won't be late. I really have to go." She wondered as she started walking whether her mother was going to grill her more. She reached for the handle of the truck door and pulled it open as her mother stepped down, lifting her hand in a wave, and she wondered about the expression on her face, whether it was sadness or concern. At the same time, the ties binding her here to this place, this property, and her family were beginning to choke her.

She was five minutes late as she pulled up to the diner. She parked in front and wondered whether he'd still be there. She stood in the doorway and saw Peggy, one of the waitresses, who was tall, slim, dark haired, and in her late thirties, also single and still looking. Taz nodded to her, taking in the half-filled diner, and then she spotted him, Jerry, at a booth at a window halfway down. He stood up and waved to her, looking tall and classy, his white dress shirt unbuttoned at the collar, his sleeves rolled up. She couldn't help staring at his chest as she walked toward him. He was not only good looking and fit, clean shaven, with dark hair and full lips, but his eyes had butterflies flitting in her stomach. They were green and bold and held something that scared her a lot.

"Was wondering whether you changed your mind," he said. Add in his great smile and she had to remind herself to breathe. She reached out, and he touched her hand again in a strong, confident handshake. He looked down at her. At the same time, he seemed to be taking in the room. She wondered what that was about.

"Sorry, just took longer than expected with work," she said and slid down onto the brown vinyl bench. He was across from her, and there was already a menu on the table in front of her. She pasted a smile to her lips and opened it, at a lack of what to say to the man across from her. "Did you order?"

"No, what's good here?" he asked and smiled again. Good Lord, he had nice teeth too.

"Everything, almost, except the meatloaf and fried chicken—or maybe I'm just partial to my mama's." What was she doing, bringing up her family? She dropped her gaze to the menu and looked up when Peggy approached.

"Hey there, Taz. Well, who is this?" Right to it, of course. Peggy's gaze was one of appreciation. Taz could feel her fingers tightening around the menu.

"This is Jerry. Jerry, Peggy—the waitress," she added, her voice sounding rough. But then, she didn't like feeling this jealousy for a man she didn't even know. There it was again, Peggy giving him a wide flirty smile.

"Cute. You're not from around here. Why, we'll just have to keep you here, considering eligible men around these parts are as scarce as white buffalo."

He wasn't smiling as he took in Peggy, and Taz could feel him staring her way now as if he didn't have a clue how to respond.

"You know what, Peggy?" she said. "I think I'll have a lemonade." This was so awkward.

"Do you have beer?" He flipped over the menu, and Taz stared over to him as Peggy tapped her notepad.

"Sorry, we're not licensed, just a family place. We've got soda pop, juice, lemonade, coffee, tea…" She was going on, and Taz wondered whether Jerry was regretting asking her out to dinner.

"Coffee it is," he said, leaning back, his arm lifted over the back of the bench as Peggy hurried away. "So, Taz, you have family here?"

"Yeah, mother and father and five sisters—well, four who live here. My older sister, Brandyne, lives out in Montana with her sheriff husband." Why she'd added that part, she didn't know. "So tell me about yourself, Jerry. You were just passing through?"

"I am passing through still," he said. "On my way home to Denver."

She nodded and wondered whether he always asked women out in strange places. Was this something he did, and then he'd be in his car on his way, or did he want something? "Denver, never been. So what do you do in Denver, Jerry?" She took in his watch, its simple design, classy and expensive. The way he dressed also said he was well off.

"You could say I have my own business, security. What about you, Taz? You're a paramedic, saving people. You probably have a lot of stories."

The waitress brought his coffee and her lemonade.

"Thank you, Peggy," Taz said.

"Don't mention it. You all decided what you want to order?"

Of course she didn't have a clue, even though she knew the menu inside and out. "Any special tonight?" she asked as she glanced over to Jerry, who opened the menu and seemed to take it all in.

"Chicken fried steak with greens, biscuits, and gravy."

She slid the menu to the side of the table. "Sounds great."

She wasn't sure what she saw in Jerry's expression—humor and something else. "I guess low fat probably isn't on the menu," he said. She wasn't sure what to say, and he lifted his hand as if he were the only one who'd gotten the joke. "I'll have the steak, rare, with a side of salad."

Taz watched as Peggy walked away, and Jerry said, "So how do you like being a paramedic?"

What could she say? She loved being needed, helping, and even though she'd never admit it to anyone, she loved the hero worship that came at times from saving a life. "I love it some days, but one day is never the same as the next. It's not all glory, but I like helping people, making a difference." Enough about her. What about him, mister mysterious, just passing through? "So what kind of security did you say you do?" There were all types, and he looked as if he didn't do the easy kind.

"People security. Big names, politicians, those in the public eye or in positions where public scrutiny brings challenges."

Wow, even more impressive.

"In Denver?" she said. "Wouldn't have thought there'd be a need there."

Again he smiled. "There's always a need everywhere. But again, five sisters, so six of you? That's an impressive family."

She shrugged. "I guess. So where's your family, Denver?"

He was just staring at her. In the green of his eyes was a depth she couldn't remember having seen before. "No, not here," he said. "My mother remarried and is living down in Australia. I have a brother in London, and my father is retired in Honolulu. So we all seem to have a piece of the world someplace. What about yours? Other than your one sister in Montana, they all live here?"

What could she say that wouldn't sound too weird? "Yeah, all of us still live here." Herself, Ivy, and Naomi each had their own cottage built fifty feet away from their parents' house, whereas Mason and Scarlett still lived at home. "So, Jerry, where are you staying?"

He tapped his fingers on the table, stirring cream into his coffee. "In the motel at the edge of town, the, uh…"

She could see him thinking. "The Red Dog?" It was one of two motels in town and was family owned, family run, and surprisingly nice, as they didn't take kindly to shenanigans of any kind.

He lifted his spoon and gestured her way. "Yeah, that's it." He sipped his coffee. "You didn't answer me before when I asked if there was a special someone in your life." The way he was watching her was bordering on intimate and had her squirming a bit in her seat.

"I remember I said there are a lot of special someones in my life." Now who was being coy? "My family," she said. "If you're asking if I'm dating someone, the answer is no, very much single." She held up her hand as if to stress the point, which was silly, considering eligible single men didn't happen around here. "What about you? Wife, girlfriend, significant other?" Did he have children, or was he just looking to sleep around? She was having a hard time believing a guy like him hadn't been snatched up.

He was shaking his head. "No, wouldn't be sitting here with you if I had."

Well, this was becoming even worse, a man of values. This was so not good. There had to be something. "When are you leaving?" she said. She couldn't help herself. Was this just a night, and she was someone to share a meal with before he moved on? What was this? He wanted fun, or was he just messing with her?

"Well, that depends," he said, and it sounded so mysterious.

"On what?" She swallowed as he leaned forward, his arms on the table.

"On you."

Chapter Six

He'd spooked her, and he still couldn't believe he'd said what he had. It had taken him all of two minutes to pick up something different about Taz after she'd slid into the booth. She may have a job that took her into harm's way and into life or death situations, he was sure, but there was also an innocence about her that he hadn't picked up on until he'd said it. The fact was that he didn't know why he had. Staying for her? She could have been taking it all manner of ways, and none of them good, which was probably why she'd become so quiet and had rushed off to the restroom.

"All finished here?" said the waitress, Peggy, who'd been far from shy with her flirting. She lifted his empty plate and Taz's half-eaten gravy-sodden dinner.

"Ah, yeah." He reached for his wallet as she rested the check on the tabletop, and he noticed Taz walking out of the restroom. He pulled out his credit card but then saw the amount and decided to pay cash instead.

Taz sat down and lifted her glass to down the rest of the lemonade.

"So what do you say about a drink?" he said. "Is there like a lounge or a bar or someplace to get a beer?" He didn't want the night to end, and he wanted a chance to redeem himself.

"There's the Toad's Hole. They also serve great burgers, but then, we ate," she said.

He could see her getting ready to leave. She pulled keys from her pocket—a woman with no purse. Then she lifted her hand to Peggy with a smile as Peggy took the money Jerry held out.

"Keep the change," he added before following Taz to the door and outside into the night. Kaycee wasn't crazy busy like the city, but there was still traffic going up and down the road. She stopped then on the sidewalk, a polite smile pasted to her lips as she looked up at him.

"Jerry, thank you for dinner, but I'm thinking it would be best if I just went on home."

There it was, the awkwardness.

"Taz, please, just one drink, a beer," he said, and she glanced across the road as if thinking.

"Jerry, I don't know what kind of girl you think I am…"

He reached out and touched her shoulder a second before pulling his hand back. "That's the thing, Taz. It's not like that," he said, feeling as if he were stumbling blind along a path, which was something he never did. He was determined, organized, planned, and anticipated problems before they happened, yet here he was, screwing things up royally with a girl he'd completely misread.

"Then what is it? Because inside you said staying depended on me. Really, like what, I'll hop on over to your motel room with you? Look at you. You could have any woman you wanted, or is this something you do, stop into a strange town and hit on a woman because…you're lonely or you have a wife and kids at home and you have an itch to scratch?" She was blushing, and he couldn't get over it. She must have realized what she'd said, because now she seemed flustered.

"No and no to everything. I've already told you I'm not married or seeing someone, either, and no kids. It's just that I'm here because of a meeting in Billings. I had never been up this way before, but after stopping for that accident yesterday…it seemed everything happened in that moment, trying to save the life, you stopping and watching as your partner took off on you, abandoning you. I wondered all night about the kid in the car, whether he made it. I stayed over and was in my car, about to head back to Denver, when I stopped this morning in the diner for breakfast, and there you were.

"And yeah, okay, maybe I didn't read you right, but I wanted to know more about you, and that's why I asked you for dinner. I never expected a conversation and a minute with you to affect me as it has. Why I said it depends on you, Taz, is because I've never met anyone like you, and I've met a lot of women and dated more—but you had me the moment you slid down that bank in the mud, taking me with you. I just never expected it. I've never been affected like this before, especially in my line of work."

Her expression was big. Her eyes were bold, and he had all her attention.

"You are someone worth getting to know," he said.

Chapter Seven

She'd had two beers, and so had he. When the jukebox started up with an old Garth Brooks ballad, he asked her to dance.

To say she'd never had a man hold her as Jerry did would be true. To be held so close and move to the music with a man who knew how to dance made her feel, in a nutshell, special. He gave her all his attention, letting her feel his hardness and breathe him in. He smelled so good that she didn't want the night to end. His hand holding hers, his arm around her when they swayed, and being so close to his face, his lips, made her die inside a little, wishing he'd kiss her.

He didn't. It was as if the man were made of steel, and as the night moved on, Taz found it harder and harder to talk. She wanted to freeze this moment in time, because how long would a man like Jerry hang around? He didn't live there, and from what she'd learned about him, a busy successful man, she couldn't believe there could be anything between them.

He walked her to her truck, opened her door for her,

and waited until she started it, and in every one of those seconds she waited for him to kiss her with those full lips that she swore would know how to kiss a woman slow and easy. Instead, he stepped back and just watched as she pulled away before walking back to the diner, where she supposed his car was parked. He didn't have her number. He'd never asked, and she'd never asked for his, leaving her so sad. She didn't know if she'd ever hear from him again. Not only had she not kissed him, but she was left with the feeling that she'd never see him again.

Now, as the sun tipped over the horizon on this Saturday morning, bringing with it yet another beautiful but lonely day off, Taz wanted to pull the covers up over her head and sleep the day away, sulking. Eligible men like Jerry didn't exist in a place like Kaycee. She heard voices outside, her sisters. Then a car started, and she listened to the sound, knowing it was Ivy, with the cottage behind her, most likely on her way in to work as a nurse in the maternity ward in Buffalo. Taz generally sought her out when she was working, but she hadn't seen her in over a week.

There was a honk, and she slid back the covers and stepped onto the cold wood floor, wearing only a white tank and boy shorts. She took a look out the window of her loft, which faced her parents' house, and saw her dad on the porch, dressed as he always was, in faded jeans, boots, and a striped cotton shirt. He was looking her way and lifted his mug of coffee. She lifted her hand and knew he wanted to talk. That was just what he did. Every morning at the same time, seven a.m., he was there, waiting on the front porch for just a look, sometimes, to make sure all of his daughters were there.

She pulled open her drawer and lifted out dark sweatpants and a warm sweatshirt, white with blue lettering, then pulled them on with socks. She took a look at her sleep-tousled hair in the dresser mirror before pulling a brush through it, then went down the stairs to the bathroom for a second before slipping on sneakers and stepping outside. She took a breath of the refreshing cool morning air before stepping down into the dirt, long grass, and weeds, making her way around her pickup to the house she'd grown up in.

"Good morning, Taz. Your mother has breakfast on, and coffee too."

Of course she did. Susan made it too easy for her grown daughters. How was she, a grown woman, ever supposed to stand on her own two feet with parents who hovered as hers did?

She stopped at the foot of the steps and looked up at Robert Parker, taking in how handsome a man her father was. The lines in his face had deepened from years of worry, hard work, and doing his best to keep his family together. He was smiling at her and then squinting, looking out at his bare land and the valley in the distance. It was peaceful out here.

"Your mom said you had a date last night?" he said.

Oh, here we go. She hadn't told her mother she had a date. In fact, she'd been purposely vague, but her mother was unusually perceptive and had obviously seen through the brush off. Most likely, the phone had been ringing off the hook with everyone asking about the hot guy Taz had been out on the town with.

"Went to the diner for dinner," she said as her dad stood there, seeming so calm and patient. She never could tell what he was thinking. He was a man who held everything in, and she wondered at times whether her mom was the only one who could read him and know what he was thinking and needing.

He nodded. "Who was the guy?"

Yup, someone or a lot of someones had phoned. She wanted to ask who had ratted her out, but the entire county was fuelled on so much gossip that she wondered how anyone got anything done in a day. "Someone I met," she said.

Her dad gave her a sharp look that had her withering a bit. He didn't have to say anything, because he really did see her as a teenager and wouldn't allow her to brush him off.

"He was at an accident the other night, one the side of the road. He stopped to help the kid who died. He asked me for dinner, that's all. He's probably already on the road back to Denver right now. He was just passing through, so it wasn't really a date, Dad. It was…" What the hell was it? There had been a loaded question and a lot of assumptions as well as chemistry that had been off the charts.

"Taz, men don't just ask women out and not want something." He was looking right at her again as if trying to figure out something. Then he was taking in everything else as if watching over his family, his land.

Her dad was the last person she wanted to talk to about this. She glanced over to Ivy's cabin behind hers, but her Mazda was already gone. The cabin behind Ivy's was Naomi's, but her lights were out, and her Honda was also gone. Her dad must have picked up on where she was looking.

"Naomi's been gone all night," he said. "She's putting in more hours interning at that newspaper office in Buffalo and working on a story she said had to be finished this morning. Ivy just left for her shift at the hospital. But everyone will be here for dinner tomorrow."

Her dad was watching her again, and she knew what he was saying. Sunday dinner was sacred, the one night every week when her parents made sure they all sat down together for dinner to check in, to talk, to reconnect. It was their time together as a family, and it was a dinner they couldn't miss unless they were working or too sick to get out of bed.

"Tell me about this guy you had dinner with," he said again. So he wasn't letting it go.

"Nice guy, Jerry is his name, and he was just passing through, Dad. I assure you there's nothing more to be said. We had dinner. He's long gone, lives in Denver. He helped, is all, tried to save that young man."

Her father's gaze landed on her again. "Just be careful, Taz," he added just as the door to the house opened. Her mother was there, and she could hear Mason and Scarlett inside.

Robert turned to her mother and said, "Was the guy from the accident, that good Samaritan passing through. He lives in Denver and should be long gone."

Okay, so they'd done more than discuss. God help her if she ever met someone and tried to have a relationship.

Chapter Eight

The Red Dog Motel had eighteen rooms, a coin-operated laundry, no Wi-Fi, and bad coffee in the lobby. The room was small and basic, with an older TV bolted to the dresser, a queen-size bed that was surprisingly comfortable, an orange side chair, and a tiny bathroom with a shower and no bathtub. Jerry had tossed his bag in the trunk of his car and strode to the office to check out. What was it about this place that had him taking a second look? It wasn't fancy, a small town with nothing spectacular other than the woman who'd stirred his interest so much he'd had to force her face from his mind. He needed to get back to Denver. He had a business to run, clients to see, and a team to organize.

The bell dinged in the motel office, and an older plump woman with thick glasses and strawberry-blond hair looked up. She smiled brightly, and he was stuck on the mole at the side of her lip with hair sticking out of it. It was distracting.

"Hey there. Are you checking out, Mr. O'Rourke?" she asked. Friendly, too.

"I am. Have to get back," he said as he lifted his wallet from his back pocket and pulled out his credit card, then set it on the counter. Home, work, appointment, and a lady here whom he couldn't seem to get off his mind.

"Well, thanks for stopping in. Hope to see you back this way again." She smiled. "It was such a shame about that accident, those two young-uns. They're from the other county, so we don't know them, but still such a waste." She was clucking her tongue, and he didn't want to be reminded of the scene, the lifeless eyes and the screams of the other, trapped as the life drained out of him. And then there was Taz.

"But glad you stayed to help our Taz," the woman said. "She's a good girl, that one, and I know her momma and daddy worry about her—well, about all the girls, really. It broke their hearts when their eldest, Brandyne, up and left with that rodeo cowboy all them years ago…" She was tapping her chin, and she still had his credit card. He wondered whether he was going to get the entire family history while he waited for her to run his card through so he could be on his way.

Then she waved her hand in the air. "Seems like yester-day, but sure it was about fifteen years ago, I think. The youngest, Mason, was still in diapers. Mm-hmm, no sir, not something we expected, but then I heard she called just this year and reached out, and the family has reconnected. Susan was heartbroken to learn her daughter had been dumped by that cowboy in some town in Montana on the side of the road with five kids to feed. She married a sheriff there. Susan and Robert said he's good people, but after that happened, they kind of closed ranks on the girls. Built cabins for the three eldest, Robert did, not far from their house on the huge spread the Parkers have. And let me tell you, when the rodeo comes to town, you'll not find one of the girls there. Robert and Susan put their foot down, or so they think—but I heard the girls have been known to sneak off and show up there."

Good God, what was it about small places that made people want to share everything about everyone's business?

"So Taz lives in a cabin at her parents' place—the Parkers, you say?"

The motel clerk slid his card back to him with a slip to sign. He reached for a pen and scribbled his signature, then put his card back in his wallet.

"It's quite the thing, really," she said, "but Robert and Susan said they weren't going to lose another daughter. Pretty sure that's Robert's way of keeping an eye on those girls. Can see everything they're up to. Heard you were having dinner with Taz, and dancing too? She's a great girl, and we're mighty fond of her. Single, she is, just like her sisters." The smile was still there, and a hint of something else. "Will you be back out this way again?"

There it was, and what could he say?

"We'll see," he said as the woman seemed to inch closer, taking in everything he was saying and waiting for him to share everything personal about him, which wasn't going to happen. He tapped the counter and stepped back. "Thanks again for your hospitality." He started to the door, then stopped and turned back to the clerk. "The Parker place, how far from town did you say it was?"

What was he doing?

The woman smiled brightly. "North side of town, five miles, just past the old Hayward place, with a driveway next to a faded red barn."

He lifted his hand and stepped outside into bright sunshine, a clear day, heading to his car. What would it hurt, really, to stop in at her place, her family's place, and say a proper goodbye?

Chapter Nine

Her mother had cooked eggs and sausages and had added in some home fries and buttermilk biscuits still warm from the oven. And what had she done, all the while adding how she was a grown woman and didn't need her mother feeding her breakfast, lunch, and dinner? She'd dug in and chewed and cleaned her plate, her stomach thanking her for filling it up with her mother's home cooking.

She helped herself to a second cup of coffee but gave herself a stern reprimand all the way back to her cottage about how she needed to tell her mother from now on that she needed to cook for herself, look after herself, and required a little separation between herself and her parents. It sounded good as she pulled off her sweats in her small bathroom, reached into the shower, and turned it on. The steam poured and slowly filled the bathroom, and she took in her image. It was the face of a young woman, Taz Parker, second eldest daughter to Susan and Robert Parker. She loved her parents, her family, and hadn't taken any stance for independence.

"You're pathetic," she added, knowing the boundaries thing had come up more and more as of late, and not once had she ever forced the issue. But maybe it was time for her to take a little more responsibility for herself, for her life.

She stepped into the shower and ducked her head under the spray when she heard her door open.

"Hey, Taz, can I borrow that blue dress of yours?" It was Mason, the baby of the family at seventeen, sticking her head in the shower curtain.

Another issue was that everyone walked in whenever they wanted. Privacy seemed to be something her family didn't understand. Mason's hair was a contrast to her sisters', bleached blond and poker straight to her waist, with bangs. She had her blue eyes painted with heavy shadow and globs of mascara, and they popped.

"Not my new blue dress?" Taz said. It was one she'd not yet worn, with spaghetti straps, a plunging neckline, and a slim waist, and it stopped an inch above her knees. She'd bought it on a whim, seeing date dress all over it, but dating was something that didn't happen around these parts.

"Uh-huh. I have a party to go to and want to look nice. I promise I won't spill anything on it…"

She could hear a car through the open window. "Party, what party?" she asked, and why was it her seventeen-year-old sister had more of a social life than all of them?

"From school. Patty Freemont is having a bunch of kids over tonight. School's almost over, and—"

"There'll be drinking and smoking, and you know Mama and Daddy aren't going to let you go. Are her parents even going to be there?" She didn't think so. Patty's parents often went away for days at a time, leaving their two teenagers at home alone, thinking they'd look after everything. That house was often filled with kids, tunes cranked, and the sheriff had stopped by a time or two.

"Oh, quit making such a big deal out of it. It's just a party. You did the same thing at my age. We're just having some teenage fun. So the dress, can I? Please…" she whined with a lot of exaggeration, and then she started batting her eyelashes as Taz scrubbed her head with shampoo.

She could hear talking in the distance, voices, but she couldn't make out whether the newcomer was male or female. It had to be her sister home. "I swear if you spill one drop of anything on my dress, Mason…"

She squealed, jumping up and down, and was going to hug Taz.

"Stop! I'm trying to shower. Seriously, why is it I can't get any privacy here? Everyone keeps walking in on me. I'm going to have to start locking the door."

"Sorry, but hey, thanks. I promise I'll bring it back washed and cleaned, too, not a spot on it. You're the best, Taz."

"I hear someone. Is that Ivy home?" she asked as she rinsed her hair, and the shower curtain dropped as Mason walked over to the window.

"Some guy, it looks like. Wonder who that is talking with Daddy," she said, and Taz grabbed the edge of the shower curtain and pulled it back, poking her head out to see her sister peering out the window. Water was dripping everywhere, and soap slipped into her eyes.

"Shit." She swiped at the burning. "A guy, who is it?" She put her face in the spray and rinsed off the soap.

"Don't know who, but he's a looker, from what I can see. Can't be from around here. Wow, nice car, too, a silver Mercedes, by the look of it."

Her heart seemed to swell and skipped a beat. She

nearly wheezed. "Dark hair, tall?" she asked and poked her head around the curtain again. At the same time, her sister glanced her way, eyebrow cocked and something teasing in her expression.

"Ah, yeah, to a T. So who's this mysterious guy who's right now following Daddy into the house?" Her sister was giving all her attention to the window again.

"Just someone I met," Taz said. Oh, major shit. This was crazy. She quickly rinsed her hair and turned off the shower, then ripped back the curtain to see Mason standing there, holding out a towel.

"And this guy you just happened to meet, is this the same hottie you were plastered against in the bar last night?"

Taz reached for the towel and wanted to snap at Mason before a teasing smile touched her lips.

"Sorry," she said. "Patty's brother, Tucker, spotted you in the bar, and on my way over I heard Mama on the phone with Hildie from town, who said you were steaming up the dance floor last night with the hottie who stopped to help at that pile-up. Hildie said it looked serious."

She pressed the towel to her face, dried the ends of her hair, and wrapped the towel around herself as she stepped out. "This town gossips far too much for its own good. And it wasn't a pile-up; it was one car in the ditch. And I wasn't plastered all over him!" she snapped, embarrassed she was being talked up in such a way.

Mason started laughing.

"You little shit," Taz said as her sister moved rather quickly out of the bathroom and pulled the door closed. Taz rubbed the towel briskly over her legs and arms as the door popped open again, Mason poking her head back in.

"You want me to go find out what he's doing here?"

Taz stood up and wrapped the towel around herself

again, tucking the ends in at her breasts, and she stepped out of the bathroom, forcing Mason to step back into the living room. "No, don't you dare. I'll be there as soon as I get dressed."

She had to get over there quickly before Jerry could be surrounded and questioned by her mother and her sisters, no doubt leaving him questioning his reason for showing up to begin with. As she watched Mason leave, hearing her jump off the step, she wondered how it was that Jerry O'Rourke had found her, and after how things had been left the night before, what could he possibly want?

Chapter Ten

"So, Jerry, what brings you to our neck of the woods?" Robert Parker asked. The man was straightforward, not what Jerry had expected—not that he had known what to expect as he found himself on the side road north of town, spotting the barn just as the motel clerk had said. The next driveway had a post box and a sign reading *The Parkers*, which he thought was problematic from a security standpoint. It was something he wanted to point out to Robert, how complacent it was to think a small rural town provided an automatic safety net.

"Honestly, I've never taken the time to drive through Wyoming. Had business up in Montana and thought it would be nice to drive back. Was just passing through."

Robert extended his hand to the blue floral sofa in the living room, an invitation to sit, but that was all. Jerry could sense something that screamed wariness all over the man.

"Thank you," he said as he took a seat, half expecting Robert to join him and sit in the chair across from him, but he didn't. He stayed where he was standing as a tall, slender woman whom Taz resembled stepped into the cozy living room beside him.

For some reason, driving in and seeing the cottages built close to the house and her father standing on the porch, watching him, hadn't prepared Jerry for what he could only describe as a silent, unnerving third degree. At least they had invited him inside after he asked for Taz. Actually, now he wasn't entirely sure what to expect, considering her father hadn't told him yet whether she was there.

"This is Jerry O'Rourke," Robert said to Taz's mother. "He's come to see Taz."

The slender woman was taking in what he was saying, and her expression was hesitant, guarded. What was that about? Not even an introduction.

"Jerry, can I get you a refreshment, coffee, tea, lemonade?" the slender woman asked.

"No, thank you, Mrs. Parker. I'd like to see Taz, if that's all right?" He knew she was around because he'd spotted her truck in front of the first cottage. He expected the woman to tell him to dispense with formalities and call her by her first name, but she didn't, so he was left with guesswork.

Robert and Mrs. Parker exchanged a look, still standing less than six feet from him, letting him feel as if they were about to grill him further. He heard the door clatter and took in a slender teen, with long blond hair, heavy makeup around her eyes, and skin-tight jeans. She smiled in a flirty way and took her time walking past, adding in a sashay with her hips that women often did when trying to entice a man.

"How is it that you know Taz again?" Mrs. Parker asked, crossing her arms over her chest after she sent the teen a pointed look. Her expression clearly showed that the friendliness was fleeting as her gaze landed back on him. The blonde was hovering in the background now at the bookshelf, running her finger over the spines of several books as if they captured her attention. Clever, he had to give her that. He wondered which of the sisters she was.

"Stopped to help at an accident. Taz pulled up in the ambulance and tried to help the guy," he added, but there was no surprise there in their expressions. Of course they knew. Everyone seemed to know everything about everybody around here.

"Huh" was all Robert said as he rested his hands on his hips, his expression giving nothing away. He didn't smile, his expression guarded. Jerry wondered then as he took in the seconds of silence, feeling the sizzle from where he sat, whether this was the first time he'd been grilled and given the stink eye by any parent.

Another sister, he was sure, strode in from the kitchen over to the blonde. She had the same round face and blue eyes, but her dark hair was so short she could have been a boy. However, her loose tank top and very short cut-offs showed off her long legs and curvy figure. She whispered something to the blonde, and they both glanced his way.

"And you had dinner with Taz last night at the diner and were at the bar with her. Aren't you just passing through?" Mrs. Parker asked, and it wasn't lost on him they may be working their way up to asking what exactly his intentions were, a question he'd never before been asked.

"Jerry!"

He heard her voice and the clatter as she stumbled in, wide eyed, her wet hair brushed back. She was wearing blue jeans and a dark blue shirt that showed a hint of cleavage. He stood up. Her blue eyes were big, bold, and there seemed to be a hint of panic about her.

"Hey, Taz," he said, feeling the eyes of her parents and sisters burning into him.

She glanced warily and worriedly to her parents as she stepped into the room, and he could feel everyone watching him and her. Talk about being under a microscope. What he'd have given for a minute alone.

"What are you doing here?" she said. It was the million-dollar question he'd asked himself as he made the turn, drove the five miles, found her place, and then pulled up in front of this house only to be met by her dad. Forget the guard dog.

"I wanted to talk to you," he said. He didn't like the way it had been left the night before, everything hanging, because he had to leave and go back to Denver, and he knew once he crossed the state line, once he made it home, he wouldn't come back. It was the reality distance could put on a relationship.

"Oh?" She was still wide eyed, and her sisters weren't even pretending now to hide their interest. Maybe she picked up on his hesitation, as she took in her family, her sisters, and said, "Why don't we go outside and take a walk?"

Yeah, that was a great idea.

Chapter Eleven

Even in the light of day, their chemistry hadn't dimmed in the least. In fact, walking with Jerry across the barren land, with no trees or any place to hide them from her family's prying eyes, had her completely rattled and unusually vulnerable. It was an odd sensation she wasn't familiar with, considering she'd never dated and never had a man come knocking on her parents' door for her.

"How did you find me?" she asked, though she knew it couldn't have been that hard in this town.

"Motel lady gave me directions and a backstory," he said as he walked.

She took in his shoes, dressy, nice, and wondered whether they were the same ones from the accident. He was in blue jeans and a dark blue dress shirt with his sleeves rolled up, showing strong forearms. The color brought out the intensity in his eyes. His handsomeness too hadn't diminished in the least.

"Ah, I see," she said, wondering how much he knew about her and her family. Probably way too much. Everything was conjecture in this town, though, and there were a lot of misadventures she wished everyone would forget. She had to wonder why he would even have made the effort to stop by.

"Interesting family. Can't say I've ever met one quite like yours." He was smiling, and she wasn't sure how to take that. At times, ridicule was hard to sense.

She stopped walking and glanced back at the house. Though she didn't see anyone, she knew well that from any of the windows, they would have a vantage point over everything on the property for quite a ways.

"And, in all honesty, it's the first time I've met a father like yours. I wasn't at all sure your father was going to let me see you," he added and glanced back to the house before giving all his attention to her again. "I guess maybe I can understand some of the worry, from what I heard." His expression was filled with an amusement she wasn't quite sure how to take.

What exactly had he heard? Now she was starting to worry. "You know town gossip isn't always accurate. What exactly did you hear?"

He said nothing as he took her in. His eyes flickered with intensity, and she wondered what he was thinking. "He's a man protecting his daughters," Jerry said. "I see a lot in my world, men and women, how they behave, fathers and mothers too busy with their lives and businesses, all their focus on themselves, to really know what's going on with their kids or even each other. Your dad isn't that way." He was shaking his head, looking back to the house again. "So your dad really built those cottages?" He gestured to hers and the two behind, identical right down to the furnishings, where Naomi and Ivy lived.

"He did." She glanced to the ground, gripped her arms, taking in something in Jerry's face that she wasn't sure what to make of. She shrugged then, at a loss of how to explain her dad's need to keep his daughters close. "You still haven't told me why you're here," she said, "and not across the Wyoming state line, back in Denver."

"Can't say for sure. Just found myself driving out here, wanting to see you again. I knew once I started driving and left this place and the miles grew between us and I arrived back home to my life and business back in Denver, you'd be on my mind, but the distance and work and my business would take up all my time again, and this…" He hesitated, gesturing between her and him. "This would be the end. To be honest, I don't want it to be, Taz," he said.

She didn't know what to say to that. Never before had a man been so bold as to express his interest, let alone show up knocking on her parents' door. Especially not a man like Jerry, considering where she was and the fact she was limited in her choices of available men, of which Kaycee had few under fifty and over eighteen. For that, she needed to step out of her comfort zone to Buffalo and beyond, but not with her father. He'd not be okay with that, and nor would her mother. Not after what had happened with Brandyne.

"I don't even know you," she said. She didn't know how to make any of this work. "You say you want to get to know me, but you're on your way home to Denver. You said it: You live and work there, and I live here. I work here. Or are you planning on staying?"

This was crazy. She spotted her mother on the front porch, and she lifted her hand and waved. Mason and Scarlett were there too, everyone with their noses in her business and most likely wishing they could listen in.

"I don't know what I'm saying, Taz. I just didn't want to leave without saying it, without telling you that there's something about you that's stirred my interest. I feel if I walk away from you and leave this place, it would be the biggest mistake of my life, and I hope you feel the same way. Do you think maybe we should start there? Because if not, tell me to get in my car, leave here, and not look back."

Her throat thickened, and she had to swallow hard to force back the lump stuck there, because she didn't know what to say. Allowing herself to admit that a man like Jerry could be interested in someone like her was hard.

"You're really making this hard, Taz, by saying nothing. If you don't feel the same, then just tell me. Don't string me along with those eyes. If you tell me to, I'll be on my way." He actually took a step back, and her hand shot out before she could reason and think it to death.

"No, don't go," she said. "You're right, there is something, but I don't know how it could work. I live here, I have a job, and maybe it's nowhere on the scale of yours and your business, but this is where my life is." There, she'd said it. What would he do?

Good God, this man, with the way he gave all of himself to her when he looked at her, had her feeling for a moment as if she were standing naked in front of him. She swallowed because he wasn't saying anything. "Are you going to stick around?" she said. "Every Sunday, my family has dinner together. Would you like to come and meet them?"

He winced with amusement, glancing back to her parents' house and then back to her, but he said, "Yeah, Taz, I think I'd love to come to dinner tomorrow."

Chapter Twelve

The dust in the distance was the only thing she could see now from Jerry's very impressive car, which was the one thing Scarlett, her younger sister, had commented on twice as she'd peered boldly through the front window while Jerry had coffee with Taz on the porch of her cottage—a very much G-rated version of what she'd have preferred.

Then he'd stood up, slid his hands down her arms, pulled her to him, and leaned down and kissed her lips. He lingered briefly, enough that she knew his interest, and then stepped down, his hand in hers, touching her until he pulled away. He was going back to Denver and returning in the morning.

"Seems nice."

She hadn't heard her dad come up behind her, and she jumped. The way he was looking down at her, she again couldn't help feeling as if she were sixteen instead of the twenty-eight-year-old grown woman she was.

"He is," she said, hoping that would be all but knowing it wouldn't be. She glanced back to the house, expecting to see her mother, but all seemed quiet. Even Mason and Scarlett had disappeared. "I invited Jerry for dinner tomorrow."

"So he's coming back?" her father said.

She wasn't sure what to make of the comment, and she couldn't tell whether he was happy or sad. "He is. He's driving back to Denver and returning in the morning." She had her arms crossed, at a loss of what to say.

"So what do you really know about this guy, Taz?" There it was, and not what she'd expected.

"Well, just that he was driving home to Denver when the car went off the road. He stopped to help. In fact, he was on the road, flagging me down in the pouring rain, doing everything he could to save the kid. He probably went above and beyond what anyone else would have done."

Her father nodded and was no longer glancing in the distance as he worked his lower lip the way he often did when he was trying to sort something through his mind and come up with an answer.

"He owns his company, I know that much. Security consulting, I think. Not sure of all the details, though, or what his bank account is like, if you're asking that."

The sharp look from her dad had her wanting to take that last part back. "You know you can't judge anything of a man by his bank account. Those are just dollars, and they say nothing of how he'd treat you. What do you know about this man and his relationships and how he treats people? There's a lot more to consider, including logistics. He lives in Denver, and you live six hours away. Or is that what he's expecting to change?"

Her father had asked the one thing she wasn't ready to answer.

"Dad, we're still at A, and you're jumping all the way

to Z. A whole lot of things need to happen between now and then. We've only just met and gone for dinner." And dancing and two beers at the bar, where she'd felt his hands on her for the first time, not that she was sharing any of that with her dad. "He's coming back for dinner tomorrow, and chances are after meeting everyone, he's going to think us certifiable and be in his car and back across the state line before sunset, so why worry about it?" she added a little flippantly.

Her dad shook his head. It was subtle but direct. "No, Taz. That man sought you out and drove all the way out here, sat in my living room, and waited for you. I saw it then when he stepped out of his car, the way he approached me, his determination and the fact that he wasn't looking to bolt the minute some heat was focused his way. No, that was a man who may not have everything figured out about how to make things work with you, but he's figured out one thing, and that is that he wants you. From what I saw, Jerry doesn't strike me as the type of man who lets too many things slip away from him.

"There are two types, those who want a woman and will do whatever it takes to get her and keep her, and those who aren't interested in working too hard for what they want. They'll get the woman, and when things get tough, they're the first ones out the door, which is what happened to your sister. I don't want that for you, so if you're serious about this guy, make sure he's the first one and don't settle for anything less." Then her dad hugged her and kissed her cheek. "Got to get back to the job site, finish up repairs on a drill head."

Taz watched her dad walk over to his truck next to the older-model suburban he'd had forever, and she listened to him start up the old beast and pull away, considering what he'd said and hoping Jerry was a man of his word.

Chapter Thirteen

He was home by dinner time, pulling into the underground garage of his high-rise downtown condo. His cell phone rang just as he jabbed the elevator button to leave the garage.

"Jerry O'Rourke," he said without looking at the caller ID. The elevator door dinged and opened, and he held the door for an older woman who stepped out, smiled his way, and kept walking.

"I left two messages," came the reply. "I'm not sure if you got them. The offer was accepted for the security firm in Montana, and security clearance just came back on the two new guys you added to the team, Gregory and Tim. I emailed the details to you." Ros had a raspy voice when she was tired, but she was the best PA he'd ever had. She was worth ten of anyone, and he needed to thank her more.

He inserted his key card as the door slid closed and pressed the button for the twenty-sixth floor, a two-story three-thousand-square-foot suite with a breathtaking view of the Denver skyline. He swore he could see for miles.

"I did get your emails," he said. "Sorry, actually meant to call you. Just had some hurdles come up on my way back. I'll send details to you about the jobs I've already slotted those two for as soon as I get upstairs. If you can get their client packets over to them, they can get familiarized and head over to meet them by tomorrow. I'll get you to follow up and make sure there are no hitches with the first meeting and getting started."

"Great, I'll do that for you. What about the Billings security firm? Do you want me to leave that with you?"

Acquisitions and mergers were always something he ran point on. He leaned against the back of the elevator, thinking of everyone on his team who could step up, those who could handle things without him hanging over their shoulders. "Send it to my lawyer. Get her to reach out and close the deal, and ask her as well to handle all the security checks on the remaining staff and those in the field. Send an email and make sure I'm copied on it." He could hear a keyboard tapping in the background. "And, Ros, I have to go out of town in the morning. I need you to handle the Monday morning team meeting if I don't make it back."

"Sure I can. Is this another business trip?" Of course she was curious. It wasn't often that Jerry left her to handle his meetings, but she was more than capable, being his right hand and sitting at every meeting, taking care of everything else before he asked.

"No, just something personal. I'll have my cell phone and laptop with me, so I'll be available if something comes up." That was how he left it, cutting Ros off before she could ask him anything else. He unlocked his door, one of three suites on the floor, and could smell cleaning solution, realizing by how neat and tidy it was that his cleaning lady had been there. He rested his keys on the sofa table, flipped through the stacked mail, and took in the floor-to-ceiling window and the view he loved, the expensive furnishings, light and plain and open. How different it was from a little place in Wyoming and a lady who'd caught his interest. His phone buzzed again. "Ros, seriously…"

"It's not Ros." Her voice was soft, distinct, hesitant.

"Hey, Jenn." He was supposed to have called her and had planned on it before that kid had blown past him and flipped his car, after which everything else had come second.

"You said you would call. You didn't." She sounded a little down.

He rested his hand against the window and took in his long fingers and the spot where he'd once worn a ring. "I'm sorry. Something came up. How are you doing? How did your signing go?" It was all she'd talked about, landing the magazine cover of the newsstand favorite. He couldn't remember which one it was. It was her deal, not his.

"Didn't get it." So that was why she sounded so off.

"Well, don't let it drag you down. There will be something else, something better. Just get back out there, try again," he added, kicking off his Italian loafers, which had been caked with mud and grime. He'd cleaned them the best he could. He left them in the hallway and started unbuttoning his shirt with one hand as he walked into his bedroom. He froze with his shirt half undone, seeing Jenn, holding her cell phone to her ear, lying on her side provocatively in the middle of his bed as if she were the prize he'd won.

"What the hell, Jenn? How did you get in?"

She was naked, her long blond hair tossed over her shoulder, covering her breasts to her waist as if she'd taken her time to pose. She had a perfect figure and was an even better lover, one he'd enjoyed more after they'd divorced.

He reached for his bath robe, draped over a chair, and tossed it to her.

"Hey!" She sounded put out as she sat up and caught the robe, clutching it in her hand but not pulling it on.

"Again, how did you get in?" He was standing in the middle of his spacious master suite as Jenn slid to the edge of his king-size bed. He realized it had white satin sheets, something new and not his.

"Your cleaning lady," she said as she stood up, giving him a view of her perfect body. He could see why she'd been a *Sports Illustrated* favorite for two years running. She just hadn't been a great wife.

"Remind me to fire her and change my locks," he said and gestured to his housecoat, which she was still holding. For the first time, he was feeling uncomfortable with her offering herself up to him. "Put it on, Jenn."

She gave him her pouty lips, which at one time would've had him doing anything for her. He'd have taken a step closer to her and let her sink all her softness around him, let her satisfy him before she left, racing off to wherever for some new assignment. That was what she did: She came for the sex but not the commitment.

"Don't be a spoilsport. I just wanted you to cheer me up." She was doing it again, this time batting her thick long lashes over blue eyes that didn't do anything for him now. They were a different shade of blue than he wanted.

He walked over to the dresser and rested against it, putting more distance between them. He crossed his arms as she dropped his housecoat, frowning, and instead took her time reaching for her clothes and pulling them on. "No more, Jenn. These booty calls of yours have to stop. This can't happen again. So what went wrong with the assignment? I thought your agent said this was a sure thing?"

She fastened her bra and pulled on a sheer blouse, then

turned to him, shrugging. "Said it happens. They went with a new face, a young model, someone unknown. Apparently I'm getting too old."

"At twenty-three, you're far from old. They really said you're too old?"

She shrugged again. "May as well have."

Ah, I see, all ego. "Well, maybe it's time you start looking at something else, other options."

The horror in her eyes and written all over her face had him realizing she probably wasn't ready to hear it. He thought back to the divorce she'd asked for—no, demanded because being his wife and living full time in Denver hadn't exactly been what she'd signed up for. Or so she said.

"And why are you here in Denver, anyways? I thought you were supposed to be in Vegas?" Wasn't there a new guy she was supposed to be hooked up with, too? Yet she couldn't stay away from Jerry. It had struck him more than once, her lack of monogamy, and he wondered too whether she'd strayed while married to him.

"You've always been there for me. I wanted to see you, talk to you. You always make me feel better, and you know just what to say to cheer me up." She strode to him and put her arms around his neck, pressing her perfect breasts against his chest.

He reached back, unhooked her arms, and stepped away. "Well, that's the thing, Jenn. As fun as it's been, it can't happen anymore. We're divorced. It's what you wanted." At the time, he'd been angry, hurt, but then the sex had become better when she'd dropped into town more than when they were married. She never stayed more than a day or two, and he realized she was far happier with that arrangement than with a commitment.

"Maybe I made a mistake." She was giving him that

look again, dialing it up to a megawatt, and at one time she could have convinced him of anything.

"No, Jenn, it was the right thing. But this here, you showing up for a booty call and then hitting the road, it can't happen anymore. You're a big girl, and you're going to need to stand on your own two feet."

The crestfallen expression on her face slowly turned to a frown. "You've met someone," she said, far from happy. "Who is she?" Now it was an accusation, and there it was: The girl who played with fire and could catfight better than any woman he knew believed someone was taking what was hers.

He shook his head as he walked over to the chair, picked up her purse and her coat, and handed them to her. "Someone you don't know, but she's special, so let's leave it at that, Jenn. This here is over. No more dropping in, showing up whenever you want. Jenn, we're divorced. You have to move on, and I don't want to hurt you, but this… isn't going to happen again."

She took her coat and purse and then reached for the black spiked heels on the floor before starting out of the bedroom. Then she stopped in the doorway, looking back at him. "If I told you I made a mistake and want you back, would it make a difference?" It was in her eyes, something sad, desperate.

"Jenn, you don't want me. I'm just a safety net, is all, and I've let you lean on me. I've made it easy for you to come to me for everything. No more, honey. You and I would never work. We were married for a short time, but you were miserable, and so was I, because you and I want two very different things, and marriage is different for us. I want a wife who's here, and that's not you. Jenn, go find your happiness, and I hope you find exactly what it is you're looking for. I need to be clear, Jenn. This can't happen anymore."

He wanted something real, always had, but until he met Taz, he hadn't known exactly what that meant. He'd always chased the lookers, the socialites, those who added to a man's image, making him look better by hanging off his arm.

She looked away for a minute. He wasn't sure what it was in her expression as she glanced back. "Can I call you still? We're friends. I don't want to lose that. I really do love you."

It would be easy to say yes. He knew she didn't really love him, or maybe she did, as much as she could love anyone. But he didn't love her, not like that, though she'd always have a place in his heart. Then he thought of Taz, her father, her family, her values, the closeness and how different they were.

"No, it would be best if you don't," he said, and he watched as the woman he'd thought was the one he had to have walked away.

He listened for the click of the door, knowing this was the very thing that would have had Robert Parker at his door with a shotgun in hand, threatening him to make him stay clear of his daughter.

Yeah, best keep this little surprise to himself.

Chapter Fourteen

Taz had changed three times and cursed Mason for having taken her blue dress and spilled beer on it the night before. She'd wanted to strangle her and had been tempted to rat her out to their parents, considering she was only seventeen, but she also knew that it was something they'd all done—well, her, Naomi, and Ivy. Scarlett was as secretive as she was dramatic, so Taz could only suspect in her case, but Mason was different, honest to a T, swearing to Taz she'd only had one beer. Even better, she'd used her brains and had called Taz to come and pick her up.

Except now Taz didn't have the one dress she wanted to wear. Instead, she settled on a deep green short-sleeve blouse that flowed past her waist, a pair of black cropped pants, and a hint of makeup. Butterflies pummelled her stomach as she watched the clock from her mother's kitchen. She was wearing a bib apron and rolling out a pie crust, only half listening to the chatter of Scarlett and her mother. She turned her head when the door clattered.

"Hey, there. That roast sure smells good, Mama," Ivy

said. She wore capris and a Red Sox shirt, her dark hair hiked high up in a ponytail. She kicked off her flipflops and walked barefoot into the large country kitchen, where she set a store-bought blueberry pie on the table.

"Don't you know that Taz has been over there for an hour trying to make a pie for her new boyfriend, and you go and ruin it by bringing a pie from the Food Mart?" Scarlett slid her arm over Ivy's shoulder, her slim-fitting tank showing off more cleavage than she knew her parents were comfortable with.

"Boyfriend?" Ivy said. "You have a man coming for dinner?"

Taz's fingers curled around the rolling pin, and she dropped it on the flattened pastry, wiping her floured hands on her apron. "Yes, I do," she said, now wondering about the wisdom of inviting Jerry today of all days to a dinner where he'd be peppered with questions that might have him feeling cornered, possibly hearing things about her and everyone in the family. The horror of what was about to happen finally hit her. What had she been thinking?

"Who is it? Can't be someone from around here. Where did you meet him? Name, details. Come on right now. Spill." Ivy smacked her one hand into the other, and Scarlett was right in there too, grinning and ready to spike up the heat, add in a dash of dramatics, and embarrass the shit out of Taz.

"He's the most handsome man, to die for," Scarlett said. "When he drove up here yesterday and got out of that fancy car of his and walked up to Daddy…" She was gesturing, being over the top and dramatic, when the door clattered again.

"Who drove up, what guy?" It was Naomi in a slim-fitting floral sundress, her dark hair brushed straight to her butt, and she was wearing dark-rimmed glasses. She looked pale, tired.

"Apparently Taz met some guy and he's coming to dinner," Ivy said before Mason walked in.

Their youngest sister's hair was now pink, and everyone was staring at her. She was barefoot in cut-offs and a black T-shirt, baggy and loose.

"What did you do to your hair?" Susan said. She had just closed the oven door on the lamb roast, and her hand now rested at her hip on the waistband of her jeans, her striped blue sleeveless blouse hanging loose.

"Needed a change," Mason said as she reached into the large double-wide fridge and pulled out a ginger ale.

Taz wasn't sure what to make of the cotton candy shade of hair that draped to Mason's waist. Her sister was always changing the color on a whim, but the blond had been the longest shade she'd stuck with. Before that she'd had jet black, orange, red, and then there had been the one-week reprieve of henna. She wondered what had happened to bring about this need for a change.

Her dad walked in and took in all of them, his eyes widening as they landed on Mason. His mouth made a big O, and Susan just shook her head as if to say, "Don't say anything."

He walked back out, but not before taking the beer Naomi handed him. She must have known, and she grabbed one for herself.

Naomi leaned against the sink, taking a swallow. "So spill, tell all. Come on, Taz. When do we get to meet—"

"Mr. Gorgeous," Scarlett said.

"He is pretty hot," Mason added before belching.

"Please do not do that when Jerry gets here," Taz said, hoping her family wouldn't embarrass her.

"Now you're evading," Ivy said, joining the mix. "Give details, and don't leave anything out."

Just then, Taz heard a car, and Scarlett squealed.

"He's here!" she shouted, running to the door to beat everyone, and all her sisters followed, leaving Taz standing with an unfinished pie and a panic that was just beginning to take hold.

Chapter Fifteen

The drive back to Wyoming, to the home of Robert and Mrs. Parker, had made Jerry take a minute to digest the difference between his old life and this. This was everything his life wasn't. There was family, there was love, there was commitment here that he didn't think he could have explained to anyone—and then there were Taz's sisters.

Mason, seventeen and still in high school, had gone from bleached blond to pink hair that would make any rocker happy. Scarlett, who was eighteen and finishing her senior year and who'd been eyeing him and his car up just the day before, was happy and eccentric and did her best to be the center of attention. She could have fit in well with any of the models, actresses, and prima donnas his company protected.

Naomi, one of the middle girls, a few years younger than Taz, was a journalist, and she had Taz's dark hair, but it was so long it hung past her waist to her butt. She had blue eyes and glasses, but her face was rounder, and she was a little shorter. Ivy, the nurse, was a little plumper but still had a great figure, and she had the same dark hair, her eyes a lighter blue, almost gray. She was the one who'd handed him a beer as he stood in the living room, waiting for Taz, who'd been yanked away by Naomi, leaving him yet again facing Robert and Mrs. Parker, who were both quiet and, from what he suspected, worried too. That was after he'd handed them the bottles of pinot gris and noir— one of each, considering he didn't know whether they liked red or white wine or what they were having for dinner.

"Well, thank you for having me for dinner," he said before he lifted the chilled bottle of beer to his lips, watching as Taz, panicky and wide eyed, hurried back in, also with a beer. Her hair draped past her shoulders, and her face had an innocence he hadn't noticed before.

"Mom, oven's dinging, and I don't think you want me poking around in there and ruining dinner," Taz said.

Ivy was sitting in the easy chair, her feet tucked to the side under her butt, drinking her beer and stifling a smile.

"Mason, Scarlett, come on in the kitchen," Mrs. Parker said. "Give me a hand getting dinner out and on the table. Naomi, you set the table for us and put out some wine glasses, too."

Then there were four.

"Taz, why don't you ask Jerry to sit?" Ivy said. "Dad, is there something you want to ask Jerry?"

Alarm was all he could see now on Taz's face along with a look that said she was going to kick her sister's ass. The amusement on Ivy's face said she was enjoying all of this, especially seeing her sister completely off kilter.

"Jerry, sit down," Taz said. "How was the drive?"

Boy, polite too. He didn't think there was going to be too much alone time with Taz happening today. What a far cry from Jenn.

"Heard you came from Denver and stopped at an accident, and that was how you and my sister met?" Ivy said before lifting the bottle to her lips and taking a swallow, her gaze taking in everything about Jerry, waiting for what he was about to say. He wondered for a moment what was behind the shadow that seemed to lurk in her expression.

"Yeah, on the side of the road, rain pouring down and sliding in the mud. It was perfect." He glanced to Taz, who was sitting beside him, quiet.

"Heard you do security. What exactly does that mean? Alarms, houses, locks and such?" Robert asked as he took a seat in the other easy chair.

"Well, it's a little more than that. It's about everything. Some clients want to make sure their homes are completely secure, with windows, doors, alarms to safe rooms, and we offer full client security for those who are a little more high profile or in businesses where they need to ensure safety from the public. There I employ staff who are assigned to handle their personal security."

"You mean like bodyguards?" Ivy asked and then gave what he thought was an approving glance to Taz, who still hadn't said a word.

"Well, basically. It depends on each client's personal needs, but we're responsible for ensuring their safety." He glanced over to Taz. "How was your day today?"

"It was good. Yours, and the highway here?" She was pulling at the label on her beer and seemed nervous.

"Long, but traffic was relatively light."

Jenn had called in the morning from Vegas, wanting a favor, but he hadn't called her back. He was struck with how lovely Taz was. She was pretty in a simple way, not all the glitz and flash of models or the surface beauty he'd once fallen for. Something so beautiful seemed to ooze from deep inside her. He'd never felt that from a woman before. He wanted to lean in and kiss her to say hello properly, and maybe that was what she saw he was going to do, as she cleared her throat at the same time Scarlett bounced back in.

"Dinner, everyone! It's ready. Mama said you all need to wash up. Daddy, Mama said she needs you to cut up the roast."

The opportunity was now gone.

"Come on," Taz said. "I'll show you where the bathroom is."

Then everyone was talking, and the smells he'd been hit with from the moment he'd stepped through the door had his mouth watering and his stomach rumbling.

Chapter Sixteen

J erry was dressed in new dark blue jeans that hugged his ass and a crisp white dress shirt with his sleeves rolled up. He was seated to her right, and everyone was talking and digging in. Her mom had outdone herself today with a roast leg of lamb to feed an army, sweet peas and baby carrots, mashed potatoes, gravy, two salads, pickled beets, and fresh buns she knew her mom had baked just the day before. Everyone was drinking wine or beer, and Susan had already twice told Mason and Scarlett they couldn't try a sip.

"Heard Bradley tried to get you in trouble, lodged a complaint against you for putting a patient in jeopardy," Naomi said, looking around. Taz curled her fingers around her fork after setting it down on her half-eaten plate.

"What's this?" her father asked.

"It was nothing like that," Taz said. "What an asshole."

"Taz, watch your language at the table," Susan said, which had her self-confidence taking another hammering. She could feel Jerry's eyes on her at being reprimanded by her mom.

"But the fact is that he is an asshole," Ivy said. "Sorry, Mama, but we see it at the hospital. Taz we like, but everyone knows that if Bradley is the only one who shows up to save you, your chances of making it to the hospital have just dropped by about half." Ivy had always been one to speak her mind—next to Taz, that is. With Jerry here and his attention for her, Taz was rattled in a way that made it hard for her to put two words together.

"Oh, isn't he the nephew of Buffalo's mayor?" Susan asked.

"The fire chief's son," Ivy said, "but he's related to the Johnson family, who have positions in everything in Buffalo. I think he's cousin to the mayor and has more relatives on the town council, a sister, I think. His uncle owns that gas company, and he has a cousin who was elected sheriff in the county." Ivy leaned around Jerry again from where she sat on his right, and Taz took in his expression and his cleaned plate.

"Bradley, the idiot partner who abandoned me—us, taking off in the ambulance," she said.

He nodded as if thinking. "So let me get this straight. You pull off the road because I flagged you down in the middle of a storm because of a guy pinned in a car who didn't make it anyways, and he filed a complaint against you?"

Her dad was watching, not eating, and she could see concern and thinking and something else. He said nothing, though.

"And who did you put in jeopardy?" Jerry said.

Maybe it was the way he asked that had her feeling for the first time as if she'd done something wrong. "No one," she said. "Hap, the guy in the ambulance, was stable. He had a hatchet shoved in his back, but it wasn't life threatening. Bradley just didn't want to stop and was tired of being stuck in the back with Hap—who, by the way, was stitched up and released the next day." She looked around Jerry to Naomi. "Who did you hear that from? I was told he tried to file a complaint, as did I against him, and that neither was going anywhere."

Now she was worried because of Bradley's connections. He made no secret of the fact that he didn't like her, and he was beginning to take less and less direction from her.

"My editor, who's friends with the mayor," Naomi said. "Did he really drive away in your ambulance and leave you?"

That was the part she hadn't shared with any of her family.

"He did," Jerry said. "Pulled away after Taz was on the road only for a few seconds to help. He honked the horn and yelled out the window instead of maybe seeing if there was something he could do, radio in for something and or tell her he was leaving her with no supplies, no nothing. Guess he was lucky there was another ambulance on its way, but I wonder if he'd stayed and helped the kid who was stuck in the vehicle, given him that few extra minutes, just maybe he'd have made it." Jerry had his elbows on the table, and everyone was quiet, looking to him, especially Robert, who sat back in his chair.

"You were there during all this with my daughter?" he said.

"I was, though not sure how much I helped," Jerry said. He wasn't looking at her but at her dad. The two of them seemed to be carrying on their own conversation.

"Well, I thank you for staying and helping Taz," he said.

This was the first time she'd seen anything friendly for

Jerry from her dad. It might not have been total accep-tance, but it was something.

"No thanks are needed," Jerry said, then held up his hand when her mom tried to pass him the platter of sliced lamb.

"Have some more, Jerry?" she said.

He was shaking his head. "No, I'm done. That was the best meal I swear I've ever had."

Mason had jumped up and was taking some of the finished plates. "There's pie for dessert," she said. "Taz started to make peach, but Mama had to finish it, and there's a blueberry that Ivy bought." Her thick pink hair was poker straight and bright, and Taz wondered whether she also saw the imprint of a nose piercing.

Jerry gazed over at her. "You know what? I think I'll pass right now, but maybe later," he said just as Taz rested her hand over his.

"Yeah, I promised Jerry I'd show him around. If you'll excuse us, we're going to take a walk," she said.

Jerry touched the back of her chair and rested his hand on her lower back as he slid his chair in. "Thank you so much again for a wonderful dinner," he said and then followed Taz to the front door and outside.

She listened to the sound of happy chatter, of family, and took in the wide open country from the front porch of her father's house.

"So, where to?" he asked as a bright smile touched the edge of her lips.

"To my place."

Chapter Seventeen

He followed Taz up the steps to her small porch and the solid wood door. The construction was new, the quality good. He didn't miss the fact that her father was standing at the window of the main house, watching them.

"Honestly can't say I've ever had a father watch me the way yours does. It makes me feel as if I'm a teenager again, but then, I don't remember dating anyone with a family like yours." No, he'd never had a father look him in the eye and let him know without saying one word that he'd crush him if he hurt his daughter.

Taz opened the door and, as if on cue, glanced past him to her parents' house. "He's just worried about us, worried you're here to tarnish my reputation, lead me astray, or, worse, have me packing my bags and following you back to Denver."

Did she have any idea what she was saying? He followed her inside. The cabin was cozy but open, with a kitchen, a living room with a wood stove, and stairs that went up to a loft, where he could see a queen-size bed. He could still smell the wood. Pine, he thought. Good quality and even better workmanship. She closed the door.

"You do know I live in Denver," he said. "My business is there." He stopped talking as she walked over to the fridge and leaned in to pull out two beers. She closed it and handed him one. He twisted off the cap. She still hadn't looked at him.

"Don't think that hasn't taken up my every thought since the moment you showed up here yesterday—or even the night before at the diner when you propositioned me." She tapped her bottle to his and moved around him, tipping the bottle, taking a sip. There was a small sectional in the living room, brown, which resembled a loveseat. She sat in the corner and pulled her feet up, her hand resting on one of three pillows. He stopped in front of her, looking down.

"You think I was propositioning you?"

"Weren't you?" She was nervous, and he took in the large square ottoman in front of her and lowered himself, his thighs so close to her he could feel her heat even though they weren't touching.

"I'm interested in you. More than interested, and maybe I wasn't entirely clear in my own head what I wanted, because of the distance. I just know that you're the first women I've ever met who has caught my attention quite this way. It wasn't an indecent proposition, but I did need to be clear. I want you. I want to have something with you. I want all of you—as a lover, to date, to…"

He stopped. Her expression had taken on a spooked look he'd not seen before. He reached for her bottle and set it along with his on the table next to her before moving over onto the cushion beside her, lifting her legs over his. He inched closer. He could smell her, and everything about her was sweet and simple. Even as his hand touched her leg and moved up her thigh, he could see and feel the effect he was having on her.

"I never expected to meet someone like you in my life. I made a choice yesterday morning to drive out here, which I'm very glad I did. Having dinner with your family just now and seeing you all together, relating to one another, I realized how wrong I was."

"Excuse me." She tried to sit up, pull her legs away, and he could see she was taking it the wrong way.

"I was wrong about who I thought you were," he said. "You're a grown woman with a career that's demanding and at times dangerous, yet you live here, sheltered, protected, and as fast as I want to move, something else inside me is saying, 'Slow down. Don't go too fast.'"

She pulled her lip between her teeth and reached out, resting her hand on his forearm, which was touching her legs. "What if I don't want you to go slow?" she said, her voice husky, soft.

He leaned in closer, her eyes going to his mouth, and he pressed his lips to hers. Tasting her, he couldn't stop himself from kissing her. Her lips were so soft that he wanted to take his time.

He pulled back a few seconds later, her breath light on his face, warm, and he kissed her nose, ran his fingers down her bare arm, feeling the softness of her skin and the way her body seemed to move closer to him. Then she lifted her arms around his neck and pressed her breasts into his chest as his hand slid around her ass, feeling her perfect roundness.

"How does this work—us, this?" she said before she pressed her lips to his again, pulling him closer, her tongue slipping into his mouth. She was cranking up the heat faster than he'd planned.

He reached for the hem of her bright silky shirt and

edged it up. Coming up for air, he pulled back just a bit. "We make it work, but I want you with me," he said. Then he lifted her shirt over her head, taking in her plain white bra, edged with lace, and cupped breasts that were even more perfect than he could have imagined. He touched one, running his thumb over the lace. Her breath caught, and her head went back, offering him her throat.

"How do we make this work? Are you moving here?" she said.

He just had to see them, the perfection, so he unhooked her bra and allowed it to drape down her arms. He lifted it away and tossed it on the floor. He lifted one breast, feeling the weight and seeing how quickly she was getting turned on.

He wanted to kiss her again before what she'd said finally registered in his brain. He pulled back, running his hand down the side of her breast to her waist, and shook his head. "I want you to come to Denver with me," he said.

Then he leaned forward to kiss her again, but the steps creaked and the door burst open. It was her dad there, Ivy on his heels. Everything happened so fast: Taz shrieked, and Jerry reacted, pulling her to him to hide her semi-naked state. At the same time, he was well aware that his very slippery welcome from her father was about to be tested.

Chapter Eighteen

"I told you I wanted a minute with Jerry," Taz said as she pulled on her bra and shirt in the bathroom. Ivy had turned their father around long enough that Jerry could reach for her bra and shirt and hand it to her as she raced to the bathroom and slammed the door.

She returned a moment later, her face burning, and Ivy wore an expression that was both horror and amusement. Jerry was now standing, hands on hips, and Taz couldn't look his way, because her father had just walked in on her with a guy who'd been, what, feeling her up?

A lock was what she needed.

"You know what, Dad?" she said. "It's not okay for you to just walk in here."

Jerry was gesturing to her. "It's fine, Taz."

"Go with your sister," Robert said without turning her way, and Jerry didn't appear worried in the least. She was horrified, yet Jerry appeared ready to face her dad and accept whatever was coming. "Ivy," her dad finally said, still not turning their way, but it was said in a tone she hadn't heard in a long time.

"Come on, Taz," Ivy said. Her sister had her arm and somehow had her outside, pulling the door closed.

"What were you doing walking in with Dad?" Taz whispered loudly, and Ivy gripped her arm again and led her down the step and around the side, away from the cottage. She glanced back at the door.

"We all knew when you left with Jerry where you were going. Dad saw you and said you took him to your cottage. Scarlett made a crude remark about wondering what kind of kisser Jerry was, and I saw the seed that little shit planted on Mom and Dad's faces. He said he was going to go on over and check on you, so I said I'd go with him—and I did my very best to make as much noise as I could, short of yelling out, 'Gee, Taz, if you're half naked, Dad's on his way over, so get your frickin' clothes on!'" she whispered loudly and then burst out laughing. "Oh, you should have seen your face, and your guy was quick, covering you up like that. I'm impressed. Shows class. Not sure Dad will see it that way." She reached over and tapped Taz's shoulder lightly, teasingly, and winked. "Just think, twenty, thirty years from now, you'll look back on this and laugh."

Taz couldn't help glancing back to her cottage as they walked, wondering what her dad could be saying to Jerry. She still needed a moment, because on top of everything, she was reeling from what he'd said.

"What is it? You have this odd look on your face." Ivy turned to the house and back to her as if checking around to make sure no one was lurking anywhere.

"It's what Jerry said right before you and Dad walked in."

Ivy, of all her sisters, had the most expressive eyes, and when she was laughing at Taz, it showed there first and in her smile next. "You were talking? Because it looked like the only talking you were doing was the R-rated kind. He was about to have you naked and shagging in thirty or forty seconds. Then can you imagine how Dad would have reacted?"

"No… I know." She pressed her hands to her face again. She couldn't remember ever having felt this rattled and confused. And horrified. That would have been way worse.

"Well, what is it?" Ivy said. "What did he say?"

Ivy was waiting, and Taz could see Naomi waving from the porch and then gesturing for them to come over. Of course she wanted to know what was up.

"He said he wants me, to date me, to have a relationship, and I asked him whether he was going to move here, but I never thought in detail before about the logistics. He said that he wants me to come to Denver with him." She pressed her hand to her chest as Naomi jogged over in her sundress and flipflops.

"Hey, what's going on here? Where's Dad and your hottie boyfriend?"

Ivy hadn't said a thing and had given Naomi only a passing glance. "Dad caught Jerry feeling Taz up, he's now talking to him, and Taz is freaking out because Jerry wants to take her away, do all kinds of lewd things to her, and move her to Denver to be his sex slave."

Naomi's jaw dropped.

"Shh!" Taz hissed. "Seriously, Ivy, keep it down. That's not funny. She's kidding, Naomi. You know that isn't true. Well, not all of it."

"So what part is true, the sex slave or the leaving?" Naomi asked.

"He wants me to come to Denver. He didn't say more because Dad walked in, and now I don't know if he's going to walk out that door, get in his car and leave, and probably never come back."

She could feel her sisters closing in. This would change everything about their dynamic. Of course it made sense that Jerry would want her to go to Denver. It would be a six-hour commute here to visit, and where would he stay? Their relationship would be doomed before it began. Maybe it was a moot point, though, and he'd realize she was more trouble than she was worth.

"Oh my God, you two, stop looking at me like I've lost my mind," Taz said. "I don't know what I'm going to do. He just asked, I don't know, and now he's with Dad. For all I know, that may be the last straw. I mean, seriously, how many twenty-eight-year-old grown women have fathers as protective as ours? He may just decide to be on his way." Her heart ached even thinking it. It couldn't happen. *Please don't let it happen.*

"You seriously think that man in there is going to cut and run?" Ivy leaned in, and Naomi appeared as if she were going to laugh.

"Well, aren't you truly a mess? You're in love with him," Naomi said.

Ivy was nodding in agreement. "Taz, that man in there is standing up to Dad for you, not that Dad could kick the shit out of him, but even I saw from the moment he arrived that Jerry has eyes only for you."

"What do you suppose Dad is saying to him?" Taz said.

Naomi was looking toward the cottage with that overly interested look she got when a story was too good to walk away from. "I don't know. You really think that?"

Taz didn't know who to answer first.

"Oh, Taz, this is going to be so much fun," Ivy said, "watching you with a guy who's put his brand on you. That guy in there seems so much like a man who decides what he wants and then gets what he wants."

Naomi was nodding in agreement. "And what do you

say we place a bet on how long it is before he has Taz packed up and shacked up in Denver with him?"

Seriously, she couldn't believe her sisters.

"Eight days," Naomi said, sticking out her hand.

"Six," Ivy said after only a moment of what appeared to have been careful consideration. "And the loser has to treat the winner to a weekend in Cheyenne at that new resort."

Both her sisters spit in their hands and then shook on it. "Deal," they said.

Chapter Nineteen

J erry took in everything in Taz's small cabin. It was a cute home for a single or a couple—rustic, cozy, and inviting except for the father standing across the room, maybe ten feet from him. Everything about his body language screamed that he wouldn't be pushed around and wouldn't stand for anything happening on his property or to his daughters. His hands were on his hips, and he was looking everywhere except at Jerry.

It was a motion Jerry recognized. Robert was gathering his thoughts carefully. Jerry hadn't noticed the belt buckle on his faded blue jeans before, a cowboy riding a bronc. He wondered whether the man had rodeoed. Maybe one day he could ask. Robert had strong forearms, which he could see from where his light blue shirt sleeves were rolled up. His scuffed boots appeared to have had years of use.

Jerry felt he should say something. He thought at least five minutes had passed, but he knew in reality it had been maybe ten seconds since Taz and Ivy had walked out the door.

"What exactly are your intentions with my daughter?"

Robert said. Okay, there it was. Not what he expected, but then, he realized he was stepping into a family that had values. This was an area he wasn't familiar with at all.

"I want to get to know Taz—"

Robert cleared his throat, interrupting him, and gestured to the sofa. "Oh, I saw that much."

He was taking this the wrong way. "Rob—Mr. Parker," Jerry said. He'd almost called him by his first name. Good Lord, what was he thinking? The sharp look had been all he needed for correction. "I want to date your daughter. Yes, what you saw was personal. I wasn't disrespecting her. I really like her." He wanted to say he loved her, but it was too soon. He needed more time. "She's everything to me, and the moment I met her, I realized she was special. She's a woman I want to get to know. I want to have something that's more…not a fling." He stressed this, because for the first time in his life he felt as if he were stumbling around and couldn't put anything coherent together. He was known for clear communication and thinking on the spot in the most dire of circumstances, but not now.

"I see. So you want to date my daughter or sleep with her?"

Right to the point. Both, though the second would likely get a fist planted in his mouth if he admitted it. He couldn't help liking this man, this father who was a bigger presence than any guard dog could have been. "Eventually, yes, I want it all with Taz. I'm not looking for an affair. I want something real, permanent. That's why I'm here, and I'm sorry you walked in on what you did."

"But you're not sorry for what you did?" Robert tossed right back.

He could lie, but that would have been a mistake. This man was watching his every move, and he was sure he could read everything—a lie, the truth, an omission. "No,

I'm not. If you want to hit me for that, go ahead. But Taz means something to me, and …" He wasn't going to talk about sex or anything like that with her father, and neither was he willing to talk about his feelings for a woman he was only beginning to figure out.

"Let me get this straight. You want to date my daughter, you want a relationship with her, yet you have her nearly naked after knowing her for five minutes. You trying to bullshit me? Why is it you needed to come all this way? I'm sure there are plenty of women where you are in Denver." Robert was standing so still. He rarely saw a man this comfortable with who he was.

"No, I'm being straight with you. I want everything with your daughter, a relationship, the two of us together, not a fling or something superficial. I want something real. You can't pick where the perfect woman lives when you finally meet her."

Robert gave a hint of a smile so slight that anyone else might have missed it. "You a marrying man? Are you looking to marry my daughter?"

He had to remind himself to breathe. Everything about this conversation was hitting him like a sledgehammer: virtue, responsibility, right and wrong. This wasn't the nineteenth century, and he hadn't planned that far. He was thinking more along the lines of living together. He'd done the marriage thing once, and he would again, but he'd take things slower. "Eventually, yes."

Taz's father rubbed his chin. He could hear whiskers scrape. His light blue eyes showed the love he had for his child. "And where would you live?"

Talk about putting the cart before the horse. "Well, that was kind of what I wanted to talk to Taz about when you walked in." He lifted his hand before her father could point out how their talking was the wrong kind. "I have a business in Denver, a place. I want Taz to come to Denver with me."

Robert let out a breath and shook his head. "You want to take my daughter away, have her leave the job she loves, her family?"

This wasn't supposed to be how it happened. He needed to talk with Taz first, not her father, and he hadn't thought more about when and how. "I don't know yet," he said, "but I do know that I want to have a chance to get to know your daughter before we get to everything else."

He waited for her father to say something else, but he didn't. His boot scraped the floor as if he were about to leave, and then he walked to the door. He paused only a moment at the door before looking back. "Coffee's on in the house. I'll send Taz back in. Come on over when you two are done." He pulled the door open and held the frame. "And, Jerry, don't you hurt my daughter." He was quiet, but his warning very much hit the mark. It was clear. Jerry had to respect the man for standing up to him the way he had done. There was so much here with this family, with Taz, that he never would have believed existed.

"You okay?" Taz said as she appeared in the open doorway, looking over to him before softly closing the door. "I'm sorry about my dad." She winced as she stepped into the room, closer to him.

He couldn't help wondering where she'd been all his life. "Don't be," he said as he reached for her hand and pulled her closer to him. Then he leaned in and kissed her just once before pressing his hands to her cheeks. "He's just a father who loves his daughters. Gotta respect that."

He really needed to find a way to make this work.

Chapter Twenty

"Okay, I'll get a room at the Red Dog again," Jerry said. He pulled his cell phone from his pocket and lifted it to his ear as they walked back from her parents', coffee in hand. Ivy and Naomi called out goodnight as they headed back to their respective cabins. Her parents had, for the first time, let down their guard and relaxed some.

"You don't have to do that," Taz said. "You can stay here."

His glance to her was sharp, meaningful, and she wanted to backpedal. He pressed the end button on his phone but still held it. "I think your dad would have something to say about that. As much as I would like to…"

She pressed her hand to his lips to stop him. "Not what I meant, but yes, you're right, I'd feel awkward too. It's my own place under the umbrella of my parents. They're always here, and they can see everything. My dad and mom wouldn't be okay with it even though I'm a grown woman." She was rambling, feeling flustered. "I meant you can have my cabin, stay in my cabin. I'll go bunk in with Ivy."

The sun was setting in the west, and everything was starting to go calm and quiet for the night. She wanted more time with him. She didn't want it to end, not quite yet.

He was taking in her cabin and his car as he slipped his cell phone in his back pocket. "You sure that would be okay? I don't mind getting a room. And your dad, he'll be fine with me staying? Maybe I should check with him."

So he was still worried about her father. "We have the room here. Dad will be fine. Don't let him scare you away. He may have issues with what he saw, but I'm his daughter." She reached for his hand, pulling him up the steps and opening her door to pull him in. "I can understand his shock. Let's just say anything here has to be G-rated, but that doesn't mean it has to be that way anywhere else."

She was about to close the door when Jerry gripped the edge, holding it open, taking her hand in his. "I think we'll leave it open so your dad isn't walking over here again, this time with a shotgun pointed at me." He rested his mug on the table and then slipped his hand under her chin. Just that touch alone stirred feelings in her she'd never felt before. "Okay, I'll stay, and you'll stay at your sister's, but then we need to talk about what happens next. One of the most important things is the distance and Denver. I said I want you there with me. I told your dad, too."

Maybe it was her gasp that had him running his knuckles over her cheek. It calmed her as she rested her hand on his wrist. "Oh, he would not have liked that."

"No, but I think he understands. I have a business, and I know there's a lot to handle, logistics wise. Just think about it. Don't give me an answer now, but in the morning,

I want you to come back with me to Denver so we can have time together."

She was shaking her head and stepped back, because it wasn't that easy. "I have a job, in case you've forgotten."

"I said think about it. I know there's a lot to handle. Take some time off. I know I'm asking a lot, so don't give me an answer tonight. Tomorrow," he said as he stepped closer to her, sliding both his hands over her cheeks, holding her tight. He leaned down and pressed his lips to hers, kissed her deeply until she leaned closer, pressing into him. She could feel him thinking as he gripped both her arms and stepped back, leaving her aching for him. "I'll get my bag," he said, leaving her standing in the open doorway of her cottage, wondering what the hell she was going to do.

Her heart said yes, but her head, her reasoning, was clouded by that kiss and him and this day. Add in the chemistry that rocked her, and now all her good judgment had been scrambled away.

"SO WHAT ARE you going to do?" Ivy said.

Taz was perched on a deep burgundy chair with matching ottoman, wearing a tank and pajama shorts, with a blanket tucked around her. She took the mug of chamomile tea her sister had steeped. Ivy had put on a little weight as of late. Even though she still had a great figure, she'd gone from a size six to a twelve in what seemed overnight, and it showed more in the short-sleeved night shirt she wore, which stopped at mid thigh.

"What should I do?" she replied. A reasonable decision had to be made. "I can't just walk in and tell Clarice, 'Hey, met a great guy who wants me to walk away from everything and go to Denver with him.' And for how long?" She shrugged, because as she talked about it now, she couldn't get over the fact that there were a lot of problems with this scenario, holes and decisions they still needed to agree on and all kinds of things that could go wrong.

"There are two problems here. You're reasoning as to how this can't work, but at the same time you want me to give you the answer and tell you what to do." Ivy took a sip of her tea and made a face. "Taz, get serious. First, when have you had a serious boyfriend, a guy with off-the-charts chemistry like the one that sizzles between the two of you? Let me tell you, we all saw it today, sensed it, and watched with envy from the sidelines. Okay, I did, anyway. You as well as I know that single guys our age around here are something of a novelty."

Taz took another sip, and as she watched her sister, she saw how tired she looked. There was something else, a sadness she hadn't noticed before. "You okay?" she said.

Ivy made a face. "Of course. It's you we're talking about, remember? Let me ask you this. Do you like Jerry?"

What kind of question was that? "Of course. If I didn't, I wouldn't be over here bunking in with you when I could be getting a good night's sleep in my own place." *Or with Jerry,* she thought as her head filled with an image of waking up in his arms, skin to skin, feeling the effects of loving him. Her face warmed. She cleared her throat.

"So he's the kind of guy you envision forever with? If he left now and didn't come back, would your heart break? Come on, Taz. Simple questions." Ivy glanced away again, and Taz noticed her sister was distracted a bit and fighting to stay focused.

"He's the only man I've ever met who has butterflies punching in my stomach just at the sound of his voice. The way he looks at me has my heart squeezing and skipping a beat, and when he touches me, kisses me, I swear I can't breathe. You hear of women talking about meeting the one and how their entire world shifts, feels as if it's tilted sideways and everything they believed to be true actually isn't. That's how I feel with Jerry. He makes everything make sense and feel right, and I can't wait to see him, talk to him, be with him, and feel him…" She stopped talking before this conversation went places that were way too personal, even though she and Ivy had talked about sex and had no-holds-barred taboo trash talks that would have shocked everyone.

"You want to sleep with him, I get it. Maybe you need to give yourself permission and let Taz have a chance to explore something that very few ever find. If he's the one, don't you think you owe it to yourself to find out?" Ivy patted her bare thigh with her hand. "This girl is going to bed. I'm exhausted and have to be up early. Don't wake me when you come up."

Taz said goodnight to her sister, watching Ivy walk up to her loft and listening to her settle into bed. She waited until her soft breathing evened out and she was asleep, and then she reached over and flicked off the lamp beside her, which had cast a soft light into the room. She was left in darkness except for the sliver of moonlight that drifted in through the window.

Then she asked herself, what if she took a chance and went with Jerry? What if it didn't work out? But if it did, didn't she owe it to herself to find out whether he was her perfect partner and the man she had always wanted?

Chapter Twenty-One

J erry wasn't sure what had woken him, and he took a minute to study the loft in the early morning light. A quick glance to the bedside clock told him it was close to six, and he couldn't remember ever having slept so deeply. He grabbed his jeans and clean shirt and strode downstairs to grab a shower, then rummage through Taz's cupboards and make coffee.

Before he could do so, he heard the shower as he stepped off the last step. The bathroom door was closed. Here he was, standing in just his underwear. When had she snuck in? It had to be Taz. He was struck by the fact that he, who specialized in being aware of his surroundings and hearing everything, hadn't heard her walk in.

He could hear a car starting outside, and a door clattered from what he thought was her parents' house. Aware of the lack of privacy, he dropped his shirt on the kitchen chair and pulled on his jeans just as the door to the bathroom opened. There was Taz, towel tucked over her breasts, with long slender legs and wide eyes.

"Good morning," he said. "I didn't hear you come in.

You're very quiet," he added, wanting to walk closer, slip his fingers into the towel, and pull it down so it pooled to her feet and he could see every inch of the magnificent body he imagined was hidden from view. What he was seeing now was pure perfection.

She swallowed and took one step closer to him, then another, until she was standing right in front of him, resting her hand on his chest, smoothing it over his skin. It was exactly what he wanted but had to stop from happening, because her touch was the one thing that would send him over the edge. He couldn't remember a touch ever affecting him so deeply, stirring his passion so much that he was having trouble remembering why he needed to stop this and behave himself.

She rose up on her tiptoes as his hands slipped around her and under the towel, feeling it fall away, hearing it hit the floor as his hands slid over her ass, her silky skin. Her breasts were pressed to his chest as he took the kiss she offered. It was instant, this feeling of drowning as he tasted her, pulling her into him, allowing his hands to trace and touch as if she were his.

Then he lifted her and lowered Taz onto the table. He couldn't stop from kissing her, running his hands over every inch he could reach, feeling her shiver from his touch. She was pulling him faster to the edge, and all he wanted to do was bury himself in her softness, in her heat, and make her his. Why was it he couldn't? He didn't want to think anymore. He wanted to feel, to connect and be with her in every way.

He kissed her jaw, running his tongue down and over her breasts, taking and tasting. They were perfect, the size, the roundness, the pink and the way she gasped and arched as he pulled with his teeth. He knew exactly how to get a woman to respond, but Taz was different. She was so much more, and she wanted him. Her arms linked around his neck, her hands running through his hair. All he could hear was her soft sighs and gasps—and something else in the background.

A crash and shriek had him breaking the kiss and moving back just as Taz jumped and pushed him off her, seeing Scarlett standing there, wide eyed and shocked. What appeared to be coffee pooled on the floor from a shattered carafe.

"Dammit, Scarlett, what are you doing, walking in here without knocking? You knew Jerry was staying here," Taz snapped as she slid off the table.

Jerry somehow got his brain to kickstart, and he reached for the deep purple towel on the floor and held it up over Taz, seeing how pink her cheeks were. Her hair was dripping down her back, over her shoulders, and he could feel the effects of having her skin to skin.

"So sorry! Oh my God, Taz, I can't believe what I walked in on—or almost walked in on. Mama told me to bring coffee over and…hey, wait. I thought you were staying at Ivy's?"

Jerry spotted his clean blue shirt on the floor and reached down to pick it up. He slipped it on, seeing the horror and panic on Taz and then anger as she glared at her sister. Jerry was trying to figure out what to say as he took in Scarlett stilling lingering with an expression he'd seen many times from women. She didn't try to hide her interest in him, considering her gaze lingered a little too long on his chest, which he knew women loved. He was strong and buff, and he spent time, along with his security detail, training with weights, boxing, fighting, staying loose on his feet. Scarlett was young and naive and was playing with fire. Robert needed to sit his daughter down and have a talk with her.

He remembered well what Jenn had said: A fighter's body is something of a work of art, and Jerry's was one she'd never tire of. Apparently Scarlett's interest in him was more than a little suspect. He buttoned his shirt and then took in the shattered glass. Scarlett was still there in the doorway. This was way past inappropriate and was treading into territory that could bring a rift between the two sisters.

"Go, Scarlett, now." Taz jabbed her finger to the door, and Jerry started around the table when Scarlett bent down to pick up the glass.

"Ouch!" she cried out, and blood pooled on her finger. Standing up, she held it out to Jerry.

He took in the cut and didn't miss Taz coming closer. "Stay back," he said. "There's glass here. Taz, do you have a broom, a dustpan?"

Of course, he was barefoot too. He took in Scarlett and wondered whether she had a clue what she was doing—teasing, flirting. Her skin-tight shorts and the cut of her T-shirt left little to the imagination, and she was edging closer, leaning into him. He stepped back.

"By the fridge," Taz said as he let go of Scarlett.

His eyes went right to Taz, and her expression let him know she'd figured out exactly what her sister was doing. Scarlett sashayed across the floor and over to the sink, where she turned on the tap and stuck her finger under it.

Jerry motioned Taz back, then took the broom and swept up the shattered glass as best he could amongst the pooled coffee. He spotted the garbage can next to the door and dropped the glass in.

"Here." Taz stepped closer and tossed a towel over the coffee to soak it up, then bent down, still in the towel. As she wiped up the spill, the edge of the towel barely covered her bottom. He blew out a hard breath.

"Check your sister's finger," he said quietly. *And then get her the hell out of here and on her way!* The last thing he wanted was for him to be the reason problems developed between sisters, even though Scarlett was the one in the wrong. She was young and obviously didn't understand that going after another woman's man, especially her sister's, was about as taboo as it got.

Then Taz gasped, which had Jerry turning around to see Robert Parker in the doorway, standing there, taking in the room, Taz, him, and Scarlett. The expression on his face gave nothing away, but Jerry knew he was seeing a man with questions—and maybe a man who didn't like whatever was happening here under his nose.

Chapter Twenty-Two

This was worse than she could have imagined. Her father was standing in the doorway now, and disappointment was all she could see in his expression. Then he looked past her to Jerry as she slowly stood up.

"Scarlett, your mother wants you back at the house," Robert said. "You have things to do to get ready for school." He didn't look at Taz as he waited for Scarlett to move over to him and past him, out the door.

Taz couldn't help the anger that had her wanting to wrap her hands around her little sister's throat and choke her. At the same time, she was feeling so many things, from dissatisfaction to shock to everything. She wanted Jerry, but at the same time she felt invaded, with no privacy, knowing her family would never allow them any time alone.

"Dad…" she started, but she stopped when his gaze landed on her, so controlled, with nothing happy there. She could see emotion and questions and quietness in her father that unsettled her and left her stumbling a bit, at a loss of where to start.

She heard Jerry clear his throat and felt him step up behind her before his hand rested on her bare shoulder. Her father's eyes zeroed in on it as if the man were touching something he had no right to, but Jerry left his hand there and in fact squeezed, a motion of support she hadn't expected. He stepped closer, and she sensed the moment his other hand touched her as if to put her behind him.

"I'm not sure what this is," Robert said, "but you're right, Taz. You're a grown woman, and this here is your guy. I see that."

She wasn't sure what else he wanted to say, and she was embarrassed, because she realized the implication. Her dad thought she'd been here last night, slept with Jerry. Even though that was exactly what she'd wanted to happen, it hadn't, because she respected her parents and knew they wouldn't be okay with that.

"Look, Dad, I'm a grown woman, but I'm also not Brandyne." The moment she said it, she realized she'd just pulled the elephant into the room, the one responsible for the overprotective shroud they'd all been living under. "She made a mistake, we all know that, but I'm twenty-eight, and it's time I stand on my own two feet."

Her father said nothing, and she could see the love he had for her and her sisters. "I know you're not your sister," he finally replied.

She nodded and glanced up at Jerry, who she could see thinking, considering, maybe wondering what the story was. He knew some, just not all of what had happened. "Jerry has asked me to go to Denver with him, and I thought about it last night." She didn't look away from Jerry as she said it, because she wanted him to know how much she meant it. "I've decided I'm going."

He seemed to get it, as a smile touched the edge of his lips. "We'll come back often," Jerry said. "I promise you I'll bring your daughter to visit." He slid his arms around her now as if he had every right.

When Taz looked back at her dad, what surprised her was his amusement and something else she'd never expected: understanding. "Well, you'd best get dressed and tell your mother," he said. Then he looked over to Jerry. "You make sure you do bring her back to visit, and often."

Then he left, pulling the door closed.

She stood there for a minute in shock, because that had been way too easy. That kind of acceptance and ease, sending her off with a man, she'd never believed her dad would have done it. She turned to face Jerry, who had a lightness in his eyes and was shaking his head as if he too couldn't believe what had happened.

"You really meant it?" Taz said. "You want me to go with you back to Denver?"

He stepped closer, stroking down her wet hair, and she couldn't keep from turning into his hand, seeking more of his touch. "I thought I would have a bigger fight to convince you and your father. I was sure he'd never allow you to leave, but I'm glad. I also realized he just wanted to make sure I'm all in for you, that I'm not going to cut out on you, that I'm willing to do what it takes to get you, to keep you, for you to be mine. He just wants you to be happy, and he already made it clear that if I hurt you, he'll kill me." He laughed, maybe at the expression on her face. "He's a good man, your father. Your family is remarkable, and…" He stepped in closer, pressing his body to hers as she draped her arms around his neck. She ran her hands into his hair as she felt his hands slide over her curvy butt, pulling her even closer so she could feel every hard part of him. "You are mine," he said before he lowered his head again, taking her lips, kissing her, tasting her, loving her.

IT HAD BEEN three days since her father had walked in her cabin and she'd decided to move to Denver. She'd quit her job as the town's only EMT and had been assured they'd have a replacement right away, even considering her short notice.

She'd said goodbye to her sisters, to her mother and her father, as Jerry loaded up the last of her suitcases in the back of her pickup. His car was already back in Denver, and he'd had a colleague drop him off so he could drive with Taz to take her back to his place.

He stepped into the cottage where she was taking a last look around, breathing in the last of a place she'd lived her entire life. She couldn't talk because the emotion was choking her, so she forced herself to swallow as he stepped in closer again.

"You okay?" he asked. He was sensitive, the best, and she couldn't wait to be with him night and day and start a life with him. His arms went around her again, and she felt him, his abs against her, his chest pressing into her breasts, making her want him so badly she thought she'd die from it. So she pulled in a breath and went to ease back as he kissed her again.

His cell phone rang, and he groaned as he pulled away. He lifted it from his pocket. She wasn't sure what she saw on his face, but he stared at the phone, not smiling, nothing. It was an expression that was cold and unwelcome, and she watched him hit *Decline*. The phone stopped ringing.

"Who was that?" she asked, and he took a second

before drawing a breath, his gaze flicking up and over to her. It was a moment before he shook his head.

"It was no one, not anyone important, just someone from the past." He slipped his phone back in his pocket and reached for her again. "But you…" he said. "You are very much my future."

Chapter 23

Hitting the city limits of Denver just before rush hour had still added half an hour to their commute to an already busy downtown, Jerry realized as he and Taz pulled into the underground parkade and he backed into the empty spot beside his BMW. Her truck was a basic older model, and he'd have preferred she trade up for something newer, but he'd have to work on her. He realized she wasn't a woman who went for new and flashy.

She opened her door and stepped out. As he went around the front, he noticed she was lifting one of her suitcases from the back.

"Hey, just leave them," he said. "I'll come back down and get them after. They'll be fine."

She gave him a look as she continued to lift out her wheeled bag and set it on the ground. "Or we can do it now and make only one trip," she said. As she pulled up its handle, he could see her stubbornness and independence. She went to reach for another bag, standing on her tiptoes, and he couldn't resist resting his hands on her hips, sliding his palms over the smooth denim of her jeans, feeling the curve. She had a great ass, full and firm and one he could look at all day, but he also had other plans, including getting her settled in his place and then into bed, so he pulled her back, reached for the bag in her hand, and set it on the ground before grabbing the last suitcase and lifting it out.

He took the two bags, and she followed with one into the elevator, where he slipped in his key card and jabbed the top floor button. "I'll get you one of these," he said. "You'll need it to get up to our floor."

She was looking around, standing in the back of the elevator, her lips firmed and tense.

"You okay? You seem quiet and haven't said much since we hit the city limits."

Her eyes were so intense, and he wondered what she was thinking, as she seemed to consider something and then shook her head. "It's nothing. Just that your cell phone rang twice on the way back and you kept hitting decline. I asked you once, and you said it was someone from your past, but that's all you said. It has me wondering a lot of things, Jerry, like how well do I really know you? Maybe there're some secrets you don't want to share."

Jenn was someone they needed to talk about, but not right now. "No secrets, but you're right. There are things we still need to learn about each other." The door slid open, and he waited for Taz to step out into the hallway. "It's the one on the end. I'll get you a key for it, too."

As he opened the door to his condo, he could smell its freshness and a lingering scent of garlic and spice. He took in Taz's expression as she walked in behind him. She was quiet, and he could see an unease come over her. "Leave the bag and let me show you around," he said. It was a second, he noticed, before she loosened her grip on the suitcase handle and then gave a quick nod.

"Sure." She settled her purse on the suitcase and went to slip off her sneakers. Yeah, she was uncomfortable, big time.

He waited a second and then held out his hand, and she slipped hers into it. "This is the living room, really the selling point of the place. You can see the skyline for miles."

His place had an open concept, and they walked two steps down into the living room. The dining room was off the kitchen, open, with formal seating he'd never used.

"This is big, nice," she said, and he watched as she took in the rooms and then the kitchen. It was a chef's dream, he'd been told, with every appliance, a gas range, and free and uncluttered counter space. A pot was sitting on the stove.

"I like it," he said, lifting the pot and sniffing the spicy Bolognese his housekeeper had left warming for him. "Well, dinner is ready. We'll just need to put on some pasta and a salad, maybe open a bottle of wine."

"So who made the sauce?" Taz said. She dipped her finger in the pot and licked it off, her deep blue eyes questioning. Then she stepped away, running her hands over the counter and moving through the kitchen.

"My housekeeper, Shay."

She kept walking and stopped again. What was she thinking? "You have a housekeeper who cooks for you?" she said and pressed her hands to the counter, leaning in. He sensed so much of a block between them. How could he erase it?

He moved around the counter, stepping closer. "I do. I can afford it, and with the hours I work, I'm not interested in cooking. She makes my life easy, keeping my place neat, dinner on, and she keeps the fridge stocked, as well, just in case you're wondering."

She nodded, flicked her gaze away, and said nothing for a second. "So how would I fit in? Maybe I should have asked before."

Oh, okay. "You're not here to cook and clean. You're my girl. I want you living with me. There's no role. Shay is here to make things easier. Is this an issue?" he asked. He could see her considering before she shrugged.

"Just nothing I'm used to. I'm not sure how comfortable I am having another woman here…"

"She's not another woman. She's older, married, and she's my employee who works for me. You don't." He stepped closer again, and she had to look up to him. He reached over and slid his hand over her shoulder, resting on her jean jacket, feeling how tight she was. There were so many firsts he wanted to reach with her, including spending their first moments here touching, exploring, and seeing every part of each other. The clothes had to go. He slid his hand down and into hers, linking their fingers and pulling her with him.

"Where are we going?" she asked, following him out of the kitchen, over the granite floors, their footsteps echoing as he took her to the stairs.

"To show you the most important room," he said. "My bedroom."

Chapter 24

J erry's place was nothing like she'd expected—not that she'd had any idea of what to expect. Somehow she'd envisioned something simpler, like a nice condo with two bedrooms, not the massive penthouse suite she was in. The living room alone was larger than her cottage, with granite floors, floor-to-ceiling windows, and two white fashionable sofas. Everything seemed pricey, all glass and metal, decorated in a way that showed his high-end taste.

Even the bedroom, one of four on the second floor, was huge, with a king-size bed. The room was done in rose and cream—not frilly, but not the masculine bachelor pad she'd envisioned. This was far from simple and screamed expensive. It made her uneasy.

The view from the bedroom was the same expansive skyline. She wondered where the drapes were or even blinds to keep out the light when sleeping, but she noticed what looked like window coverings that would drop down at the flick of a switch.

She stood there facing Jerry and feeling unusually shy. At the same time, she was hit by a wave of panic. Was she completely insane? As her head started to see all the problems, she realized that maybe she hadn't thought anything through. She'd quit her job to move away from her family and in with a guy she barely knew. Even though there was attraction between them, a chemistry that made her feel as if she had to have him now, as she stood there feeling his eyes on her, she couldn't help freaking out at the thought that she'd done something she wasn't ready for.

She felt his hands on her shoulders, slipping down and sliding around and over her breasts, her stomach, just holding her. She leaned back into him.

"I can see you're starting to freak out a bit. You're so tense," he said as he held her close, which eased some of her panic.

"Jerry, I…"

"Shh, how about we take a minute to just be together?" His hands slipped over her shoulders again and hooked onto the edge of her jean jacket to pull it off, peeling away one of her layers. She stepped away and looked at him as he tossed it onto the padded bench at the foot of the bed. It too was tasteful, a French design. Everything was so neat and tidy.

His eyes again had her swallowing as he stepped closer, lifting his hand to her cheek. "What's going on in that head of yours? I noticed as soon as we walked in, and it can't be because of my housekeeper," he added. He was holding her like a treasure, his thumb rubbing her cheek, and she took him in, trying to piece together everything about him.

"You have so much more than I thought. I didn't expect anything this big. This place is huge, not something me or my family could ever afford—and no, it's not really about the housekeeper, although I am surprised. Never known someone to have one, but you have her come in and cook too, and then there's all this. I didn't expect how expensive it looks. I didn't take you for a guy with this amazing decorative skill. Everything is tasteful, and all the detail, from the vases, the art, the sculptures… There's so much I don't understand." It was nothing she'd have ever chosen and not the kind of thing she'd have spent time on. To her, a home was about the simple things, the basics.

"And this bothers you?" he said. He was looking around, and she wasn't sure what she saw there. He shrugged. "Change whatever you want to, whatever you want. Not a big deal to me."

She didn't know what to make of his comment.

"The only thing I care about is you and me here," he said. "If something bothers you, change it, or say something and I will." He was standing in her space, closer now, his fingers threading through her hair. He held her face still and then lowered his head to kiss her, and it was slow. For the first time, as she allowed herself to sink into that kiss, she wasn't worried about privacy or about anyone walking in on them.

"I want you right now," he said as he walked her back to the bed and lowered her onto the mattress.

She could feel him pressing into her. She wanted him, and although she hadn't thought too hard about all of this, moving here and being here with him now, she thought she'd die without his kiss, his love, feeling him inside her.

She reached for the buttons of his shirt, and she just wanted to feel, to not think anymore. She was lost in the sensations as he peeled away her clothes, allowing him to explore and touch, to just feel every inch of her. With each kiss and sensation she'd never felt before, she was drowning with need. As he pressed into her that first time, the discomfort lasted for only a second. He stilled but kept kissing her, moving deeply, gently. She knew in that moment that it wasn't a mistake. None of this was a mistake, because being here, feeling this with him, she had never felt so right.

Chapter 25

She was in his kitchen, singing and humming, wearing just his T-shirt. He could smell bacon cooking. When she noticed him, she smiled brightly, the morning sun streaming in. For the first time, her expression was relaxed.

"What are you cooking?" he asked as he stepped into the kitchen and slid his hands over her waist and downward, feeling her curves. He linked his arms around her waist, holding her to him, and kissed the side of her head, seeing eggs sizzling in a frying pan.

"Bacon, eggs," she said. The toaster dinged behind him, and she moved away. "And toast. Hope you're hungry, because I'm starved. Oh, and I put that spaghetti sauce in the fridge, considering we didn't get a chance to eat a thing last night." There was some color on her cheeks, and this time he just stayed where he was and took her in, trying to figure out how he'd ever found her.

She was lifting toast from the toaster and then buttering it. "Grab two plates for me," she said as she hurried to the stove and flipped over four eggs, then turned the sizzling bacon, which appeared done.

"Sure," he said. "So…we should talk about last night." He lifted two deep burgundy plates from the cupboard. They were cut with a diamond design at the edges, the set Jenn had ordered. He hadn't thought much of them until now.

He set the plates beside the stove and took in how quiet Taz became as she lifted two eggs onto each and added toast, then bacon. She rubbed her hands together. "Okay," she said and pulled two forks and knives from the drawer. Jerry took the plates to his round dining table, which was already laid out with ketchup, peanut butter, raspberry jam, two mugs, his French press of coffee, and a carton of orange juice. He put the plates down, and she took a seat next to him.

"I guess I just assumed a lot of things," he said, "but never in my wildest dreams could I have imagined you'd never been with anyone."

Her eyes were wide, startled. She said nothing.

"You should have told me."

The blue of her eyes appeared to darken, and he saw her anger as she lifted her fork. "Why would I tell you? Were you disappointed?" she snapped.

"No, how could you think that? It's just that you're twenty-eight, and I can't even tell you how unheard of it is to find a woman like you. I'm not disappointed—I'm happy, but still, you should have told me."

She didn't seem to get it. The confusion was still there.

"I could have hurt you," he said. "I assumed a lot of things I shouldn't have, like with birth control. I used a condom, but I don't want to forever."

"Let me assure you that you did not hurt me. It was enjoyable, quite. And I'm on the pill. Ivy's a maternity ward nurse and is big into protection. So not to worry. She made me go on it last year even though I had no prospects." She forked up a large bite of eggs and toast. "My cooking isn't that bad, you know. My mother is one of the best around, so I did learn a few things." She gestured to his uneaten plate, and he made himself pick up a fork and dig in.

"I take it you're hungry?" he said.

She rolled her eyes. "Starving. Considering we didn't come out of the bedroom all night and didn't eat dinner, my stomach is what woke me."

She was rattling along, and he stopped listening. It was killing him as he stared at her mouth, her lips, and he felt denied the pleasure of waking up with her warmth beside him in bed, skin to skin and wanting to slip inside her again. The chemistry oozed, and he wanted her again, so he scraped his plate and downed a coffee. As soon as she finished her toast and swallowed some juice, he slid his chair back and lifted her, moving the plates aside to make a spot on the table to lay her down.

She ran her hands over his bare chest and his sleep pants, pulled low on his hips. As he was between her legs, stripping her of his T-shirt, his landline started ringing. It was loud, with handsets throughout the house, but he kissed her neck and ran his hands over the softness that he needed to have again. He'd never tire of her.

Her hands were now planted on his chest and pushing him. "Your phone," she said, but she hissed as he ran his hand lower. She was so responsive to his touch. He realized the fun he was going to have, teaching her everything there was to know about being with a man. Everything would be her first, a gift. He wondered if she had any idea how much that meant.

She flattened her hands on his chest again when the

phone kept ringing. He could hear the phone calling out the caller, the number, and who it was. Jenn, dammit. He moved away from Taz and grabbed the phone before it could go to voicemail.

"Hello?" he snapped, looking back over his shoulder to Taz, who had scrambled to the floor and was now slipping the T-shirt back over her head to hide her nakedness. He wanted to weep for a moment and at the same time curse Jenn for interrupting.

"Well, hey there," Jenn said. "You never returned my calls."

He could hear something in her voice, a mood or the start of one. It was nothing he wanted to deal with at the moment. He walked out of the dining room and past the foyer to his office at the end, and he slipped inside and behind his desk. "I didn't. You're right," he said. He could hear dishes and figured Taz was cleaning up breakfast. He'd finish with Jenn and then scoop her up and take her to the shower with him. Shower sex would cheer him up and be another first he could teach her. He smiled to himself.

"Why are you being like this, Jerry? I love you and need you."

Not this again. "You don't, and you can't keep calling. I already told you this when you showed up here the last time. No more. I'm not here for you to just show up for a booty call whenever you need it. You're a big girl, Jenn. You can stand on your own two feet."

There was silence on the other end. "Jerry, that's just cruel. Who am I supposed to talk to about my agent? I think he's screwing me around and has kept money from me."

"Did he do something to make you think that? Do you know for a fact he's withholding?"

Jenn at times was dramatic and blew things out of proportion, but not with money. "Jerry, that's the problem," she said. "I got distracted and was just pulling together the royalty and commission statements for my accountant. That's when I discovered missing payments. He was getting the royalties and was supposed to take his fifteen percent, but I found that he's shorted me a lot. It wasn't anything glaring, but you know how I am with money."

He did. In fact, he'd have hung up otherwise. "Did you talk to him, ask him about it?"

She huffed on the other end, annoyed. "Of course I didn't. This wasn't just some accounting error. It's too obvious a mistake. I'm calling you first. I thought maybe you could use your contacts and find out for me, maybe trace where he has my money…"

"And, what, threaten him, or is there something else you want to happen when I do find out?" He didn't love Jenn, and he could feel the disconnect now, talking with her, even though he cared about her and always would, he presumed. He certainly didn't like the idea of someone who was supposed to be helping her, who she should have been able to trust, ripping her off.

"So you'll take it, you'll find out for me?" she said. When Jenn was happy that something was about to go her way, he could hear it in her voice, and, without a doubt, she was off-the-charts happy right now.

"Yeah, I'll find out, pull his financials, do some background on him," he said as he leaned back in his leather chair, taking in the art on his walls that Jenn had bought, one of the first pieces for him, a Kinkade that he loved. It reminded him so much of her. Maybe it was time for it to go.

"Oh, thank you, Jerry. I knew I could count on you.

Listen, how about dinner tonight? I'm flying into Denver, and we could meet and talk. I could come over...."

Oh, no, definitely not. "Jenn, I already told you it's over between us. There's no more coming over. I'll help you with your agent, but that's all," he said. He could hear disappointment in her silence.

As he glanced up to the door, he saw Taz there, holding a mug of coffee. Her expression told him she had heard, and he felt guilty for having said nothing.

"Listen, I've got to go," he said and hung up before Jenn could say another word.

Taz strode in with the steaming mug of coffee and rested it on his desk, taking a moment and then another to gather her thoughts. "I thought you'd like another coffee, so I poured you one. I wasn't eavesdropping." Her gaze flicked to his then, and it was so much like getting punched, what he saw there. "Who's Jenn?"

Yeah, she'd heard, and for the first time, he felt as if he'd done something he shouldn't have.

Chapter 26

Pulling deep within herself to find the calmness to deal with difficult situations came naturally to Taz. Standing before his desk, she linked her fingers together, fighting the urge to wrap her arms around herself, feeling more exposed than she was comfortable with. It was an awful raw feeling that scraped inside her, stealing her joy and excitement.

What made it worse was that Jerry was now standing, and his expression appeared guilty. She knew guilt, having grown up in confined quarters with five sisters. One of them had always been caught up in someone, something, or some situation, trying to pull one over on their parents, to hide something they shouldn't have done. She had very much that same feeling now, and she didn't like it. She had nothing of her own to fall back on—her home, her family, her job. She was seeing this situation with both eyes wide open.

"Who's Jenn?" she said again. Her voice sounded off.

He wiped his face, the dark whiskers giving him a sexy morning shadow. His hair was a mess, but instead of making him look rough, it had the opposite effect, leaving her wanting to move closer and slide her hands over his shoulders, let him hold her. But she wouldn't, she couldn't. She wasn't made that way. She could never be someone like that.

"She's my ex-wife," he said.

For a minute, she felt as if the floor had given way beneath her. At the same time, she felt how tight her stomach had become, and she reminded herself to breathe. "Didn't know you were married," she said. "Why wouldn't you have told me you were married? It's something I think you should have mentioned."

Had she even asked? She'd asked the other things: Was he married? Did he have a girlfriend? Was he involved with someone? Why had his conversation with the woman sounded a lot like something was still active between them? "Why are you talking to her if you're divorced? It sounded like there was something more."

He started around the desk, and she took a step back. "It's not like that," he said. She could see how he stopped himself from reaching for her and pulling her to him. Maybe he realized she couldn't be pacified. Smart man. Would he lie to her?

"Then explain to me what it is. Divorced means you were once married, and it's something you should have mentioned. Right now I'm feeling like if I don't ask the right question, I won't get the answer, and that to me seems so much like evading, like lying. I don't want that. I can't live that way. I won't," she stressed, her hand pressed flat to her chest as she leaned in but kept her distance.

He took another step, lifting both hands in the air. "Got it, and it wasn't an omission. I'm not married or involved with Jenn anymore. I told her to stop calling.

We're through and divorced. She called for a business reason."

The moment he said it, she wanted to yell at him what bullshit that was. "I heard you say there's no more coming over. What did you mean by that? You see her? She comes here? Why are you helping out your ex-wife, doing business together?" She wasn't sure how to feel, but she definitely didn't like the wave of jealousy that crept in. It was a feeling she hadn't felt often, and she didn't care to have any part of that in her life.

"Look." He settled back, leaning against his desk, his hands gripping the edge. "She's got a situation I said I'd look into for her. I'm assigning it to one of my employees. It will be handled, and then I promise you there'll be no more contact."

It wasn't lost on her that he hadn't answered everything. "Has she been here? Are you sleeping with her?" Why she'd asked that, she wasn't sure, but it was a nagging question that had popped up, and she needed to know.

"She has, but there's been no one since I met you. I didn't lie about that. She's come by, and the last time I made it clear she can't anymore," he said.

She watched the green of his eyes, which seemed sincere, as if he meant what he'd said. She knew lying, and she was sure he was being truthful. "She's in love with you still."

He shook his head, and the smile that touched his lips seemed more sarcastic than amused. "I guarantee you she doesn't love me, she loves herself. She only sees me as a safety net, that's all, and, just so we're clear, I'm not in love with her."

She wondered. She hadn't met the woman, and as she looked around now, she realized maybe all the touches here in this place weren't from Jerry. "Did she live here with you? Did she furnish this place?"

He shrugged. "Yes. Doesn't mean much. It's not my taste, but she did it all. Why does it matter? She doesn't live here—you do, I do."

She didn't want to live in another woman's shadow. "Did she buy the art, the bedding, the dishes?" Was everything here his ex's?

"Yeah." He shrugged. "Again, it's not my taste, not my style. Change whatever you like. It's not a big deal to me, but you are, and if you want something gone, just do it. Tell me."

"So you're not attached to any of this?" She gestured to the walls, the artwork, the metalworks, the cabinet.

He pushed away from the desk and moved to stand right in front of her, putting his hands on her shoulders. This time she didn't step back. "I told you, you're what matters. Us. She's gone. I'll help her with her business problem, but that's it. There's nothing between her and me. It's over. We're divorced. We're not involved. I don't want her, I want you," he said, running his hands over her shoulders and to the sides of her head, holding her. He lowered his head to hers, close, as if he was waiting for her okay to touch her, to kiss her.

"Okay," she whispered.

He scooped her up in his arms and walked out of his office, and she squealed as he carried her into his bathroom as if she weighed nothing. He put her down there and turned on the shower. As he stepped out of his pajama bottoms and stood before her, his amazing body called to her, and she lifted the T-shirt over her head, dropped it to the floor, and took his hand, letting him lead her into the shower.

Chapter 27

It was Monday morning. Jerry had left the building at seven a.m. for what he'd said was his weekly meeting after two days of the only and best sex she'd ever had. She was both exhausted and sated—and a little sore, even though she wouldn't admit it to Jerry. It had been a weekend of a lot of things to overcome, including his ex. Just learning about her had set her teeth on edge.

Even though he'd assured her that this woman he'd once been married to and shared a close connection to wasn't a part of his life anymore, she couldn't help wondering if that was possible. After being that intimate and sharing the closeness of marriage, could he simply pull Jenn out of himself? She didn't understand how, but then, Jerry really was a first for her in so many ways. Maybe it would help if she put more of her own touches into this condo. She had money saved and had put some thought into it, but she had other firsts she needed to do today. Foremost, she needed to find a job. She had an interview lined up at one of Denver's stations for a part-time EMT position. This would be her foothold into the city, a bigger department, and situations possibly far greater than what she'd encountered around Kaycee. She was excited even though Jerry had been less than enthused at the idea.

She used her key card and rode down the elevator to the parking garage, which was half empty now. She eased her truck out of the tight space and into the heavy traffic. It took only twenty minutes to drive to Station Eleven and find parking on the next street over. She was five minutes early when she pulled open the front door and saw two fire trucks and one ambulance in the open bay. A uniformed guy was washing down one of the firetrucks, spilling suds on the concrete driveway, and she could hear talking and joking from other voices in the back. She stood at the empty counter and caught the eye of a man of average height, with dark hair that was thinning in the front. He had a solid build and a nice smile.

"Can I help you?" he asked as he walked over in his dark blue uniform. The nametag on his chest read *Captain Remmie*.

"I'm Taz Parker, Captain Remmie. I spoke with you yesterday regarding the part-time EMT position."

He smiled even brighter. "You're punctual. I like that," he added, extending his hand in a firm handshake. Nice. She liked him. "Come on back. Do you want some coffee?"

He walked her back and past a room holding at least ten or so emergency personnel, two playing ping pong, another reading a paper, and a few others lingering around.

"Hey, Cap'n," one of them called out. Seeing Taz, he added, "Is that the new recruit?" He was a light-haired man with blue eyes, a flirty smile, and no ring.

"This is Taz Parker. She's applied for the part-time

paramedic position. She's from up in Johnson County, Wyoming, working out of Buffalo."

She was impressed. He'd done his homework. She wondered what kind of recommendation Clarice had given her.

"Taz, pleasure," the man said. "The name's John. You'll be working with me, filling in for Amy. She's on maternity, even though she says she's coming back. That's her husband in back. Hey, Steve, this here is Taz, who's taking over for your wife!"

Taz wanted to clarify that she was only here interviewing and hadn't been offered anything, as everyone was now watching her and calling out as Steve, a tall handsome man with a bald head, a stud in his ear, and a tattoo on his forearm of some bird she couldn't quite make out, shook her hand. He had nice eyes, too—light brown, almost golden.

"Great to have you here, Taz. You'll likely meet Amy at some point, as she hasn't quite got the memo she's not working anymore."

The captain chuckled under his breath, "She's got how long until she's due?" he asked.

Then another two firefighters stepped over and introduced themselves. Both were really good looking, and she had the sense that everyone was part of a really big family.

"Another eight weeks," Steve said. "She's going stir crazy. It's our first, and she's loved being a paramedic, thinks she can do it all, but after we found out it was twins, I think even she knew that was it. After they're born, she won't be coming back. She just hasn't admitted it to herself. But don't worry." He actually winked in her direction as if it were a sure thing. "She'll come around. She does it with everything, not wanting to give up, and she fights to hold on to the very end until she figures out for herself that she's fighting a battle she didn't really want to win anyway." He made a face as if she was exasperating, and one of the guys in back added that Amy kept everyone on their toes. It had everyone laughing, including Taz. She sounded like someone interesting, like one of her sisters, someone she wanted to meet.

"So when are you starting?" John asked.

"Well, the job hasn't even been offered to me yet," Taz said. She'd never felt so much like she'd been thrown in at the deep end before, and she didn't know what to say as she glanced over to the captain, who had a light in his eyes and was covering his mouth as if hiding a smile. He then rested his hand on her shoulder.

"The job's yours, Taz, if you want it, which we hope you do. Spoke with your boss in Buffalo and got glowing recommendations from her, the volunteers, and, from what I understand, half the town, so it came down to me just wanting to meet you in person."

She didn't know what to say. This hadn't been what she expected coming down here. "Well, yes. I say yes! Thank you."

Everyone came over, introduced themselves, and welcomed her to the team. She hadn't expected everyone to be so open, and she couldn't wait to get home and tell Jerry the good news.

Chapter 28

J erry had just backed into his stall and was about to call Taz when Jenn's name popped up on his dashboard's caller ID. At least Taz's truck was there, so she'd made it back. Good.

"Jenn, this is four times today—a little much, even for you," he said as he put the car in park and turned off the engine.

"I just wanted to thank you again. That guy on your team really stepped up, and an hour ago I got an email from my agent saying, and this is a quote from the email, 'I've stumbled across an accounting error that I need to rectify immediately.' Somehow, his bookkeeper unknowingly calculated the incorrect percentage. It was entirely innocent, and he'll be forwarding the outstanding amounts by end of week."

He smiled. It had been an easy fix, and he'd already heard back from his IT guy, who'd hacked into the agent's system and then reached out to the agent to give him a very direct and clear message: Fix it or all hell would break loose, and his chances of ever picking up another client would be zero. It had apparently worked and was one more thing Jerry could cross off his list before sending Jenn on her way.

"I'm very glad for you," Jerry said as he strode to the elevator, his briefcase in hand. He jabbed the elevator button.

"So can I take you for dinner to celebrate, maybe bring a nice bottle of Masseto? We could drink it and I could thank you properly."

"Jenn, no, you can't. Do I need to remind you again that we aren't together? We're divorced. I've moved on. You need to, as well," he stressed as the elevator door slid open. He stepped inside.

"Well, I know we're divorced, but I love you, and I kind of like how things are now. I think that was where our mistake was, getting married. I felt trapped, but now things are better. Our relationship is stronger. The sex is amazing. Don't spoil a good thing." She was pushing, and he needed to get her to understand.

"Jenn, I already told you I've met someone," he said and didn't miss the silence on the other end. He didn't know what she was thinking. "She's living with me now. I'm planning a future with her. I'm sorry, but there can't be any more dropping in or calling. She's not okay with that, and she's the kind of woman I could have forever with. Do you understand?"

Again, silence for a minute. "I guess I should be happy for you. Are you sure she can make you happy, Jerry? You're an important man, busy. Is she going to give you what you need?"

The elevator slowed, and the doors opened.

"She's everything to me, Jenn, and I never expected a woman like her existed. Yes, she gives me what I need, so, again, you can't call anymore. I really do hope you find what you're looking for," he said before disconnecting and opening the door to his suite.

He was hit by an aroma that had his stomach rumbling. Dinner was cooking, a country western station was playing in the background, and the artwork in the front entrance was gone, along with the Chinese vase and crystal, replaced with personal photos of Taz and her sisters, her family. An old-style pitcher sat on the table, and by the door was a padded bench with drawers below for hats, gloves, and scarves. It reminded him so much of Taz's cottage in its color and style. He took in some of the other changes as he set his briefcase down at the door and realized all the art on the walls, which he knew was worth a lot of money, hundreds of thousands, was gone.

Taz stood in the kitchen at the stove, stirring something, dipping her finger in, and tasting. He strode into the kitchen, seeing her slimness and her curves. She was barefoot in capris and a white loose tank, her lacy bra showing. It was casual and enticing, and she looked up with a big smile as she lifted a tray of biscuits from the oven.

"You're home!" She was radiant and looped her arms around his neck, kissing him and lingering so he could run his hands over her ass and feel all her softness. "I got the job," she said as she pulled back.

"Yeah? That's great! The temporary part-time one?" he said. He hoped she'd have found something a little different, and at the same time he hoped the hours wouldn't conflict with his. It was selfish, and he couldn't admit it to her.

"Yes, but I've been assured it won't be temporary for long. Well, the lady I'm filling in for is…"

He stopped listening as she rattled on, happy and excited for something that was hers alone, and he couldn't help worrying that it would be more important to her than him. He'd been down that road before and had no desire to go that way again. He wanted selfishly to have a woman who gave all of herself to him, to their home, and maybe to their kids down the road. He'd seen her family, her parents, their life together, and he wanted something similar. He said nothing and realized she was watching him and no longer talking as she stirred.

"What's for dinner?" He leaned over and dipped his finger into the hot pot of gravy, then licked it off, tasting all that fatty goodness. "Yum."

"I made fried chicken. There's a slaw in the fridge, and biscuits and sausage gravy. Are you okay? You don't seem that excited about my job. Or is it something else? I took the art down and some of that fancy stuff." Her hair was damp on the ends, and he could smell its showered freshness.

"No, it's fine about the stuff. I told you to do whatever you want here. Did you give the art away?" He couldn't help wondering about it.

She made a face, shaking her head. "Stuffed it all in the empty room at the end of the hall with the big closet. Are you sure there's nothing else?"

"Honestly, just selfish thoughts. I don't want to share you," he said and took in the smile that touched her lips as she slid her arms over his shoulders and allowed him to touch her ass. She leaned in closer, teasing him, feeling him.

"I see. Well, the hours are only three days a week, starting at seven a.m., Monday, Tuesday, and Saturday, and maybe the occasional nightshift, but I was assured already that would only be to fill in as needed. So I'll most likely be home before you. Can you live with that?" She was teasing him again, and he wanted to strip her down right there and take her in the kitchen on the counter. He was quickly making a plan to have her in every room of the house.

As he pulled back from kissing her again, his hands trailing along the edge of her waistband, he said, "Turn off the gravy and the oven." He moved her back, lifting the tank over her head and dropping it on the floor. "I'm going to christen this kitchen right."

Her eyes widened when his intention sank in. "Here?" she squeaked as he unhooked her bra, then turned off the gas range stovetop and oven. He moved her back until she bumped the large center island, and he lifted her, setting her on the edge. He stepped between her legs, running his hands over her breasts, taking in how he affected her.

"Right here, right now," he said, and he kissed her again, tasting her sweetness. He pulled back long enough to pull off her capris and underwear and his own shirt. "I plan to have you in every room. This is our place."

The only memory he wanted to have when he walked into a room was of the many times and places he'd made love to Taz there.

Chapter 29

Her first week was over, and it was far different in a lot of ways—but the same in others—from working for a smaller county in another state. Denver had a different mindset than where she'd grown up, with a lot more acceptance of her being a woman and far fewer rednecks who believed they ruled the county. The men at the station were great, fantastic, accepting, including the two female firefighters who'd clawed their way up, but the days were far from slow, and today had been especially bad, with a drug overdose and two car crashes, one dead at the scene. There had also been a backyard fire after a young male had thought it would be a great idea to squirt lighter fluid from a can directly onto his homemade fire pit, lighting his arm on fire and causing burns to part of his face. Apparently, idiots weren't specific to her part of Wyoming.

The worst, though, had been the call to a part of town known for drug use, to a meth cookhouse, where she'd found an infant half dead. She didn't think she'd get the image out of her head, and the ER doctors had said the chances of survival for the six-month-old baby were slim. Starving and breathing in chemicals her entire life had caused all of the little girl's organs to start to shut down. It was one of those calls the other paramedic, John, said they'd never forget. It stuck with her, and even though she'd been invited for a drink with the firehouse team, she'd declined, wanting to slip into a hot bath and then spend some time with Jerry just cuddling, touching, being together, and not saying a word.

She dragged herself out of the elevator and down the hall, pulling keys from her pocket before opening the door. She dropped her purse on the bench and kicked off her shoes, taking in a large framed portrait wrapped in brown paper. She wondered what it was. Jerry must be home early, but she didn't remember seeing his car—not that she'd paid much attention. She took in the quiet and the neatness, remembering his cleaning lady would have come in sometime earlier. Maybe it wasn't such a bad thing. At least now she didn't have to clean this place. It was huge, and cleaning was not something she was particularly good at, nor did she enjoy it. That was her mother's thing, though on Saturdays she and her sisters had all pitched in to help while growing up. Having someone else do it, she had to admit, was something she could get used to.

She could hear the shower running and smiled as she thought of slipping inside with Jerry, washing his back and letting him press her against the shower wall to make love to her hard and fast the way he had the day before as the warm water sprayed over them. She unbuttoned her uniform and pulled it off, then dumped it in the laundry along with her pants and socks, followed by her underwear and bra. She strode into the bathroom and pulled open the glass door only to be hit by alarm as a woman with long blond hair and blue eyes stared back at her from where she was rinsing out her hair.

Taz reached for a towel and wrapped it around herself—horrified, terrified, and looking around for the phone. "Who the hell are you? How did you get in here?" she yelled, backing away.

The woman turned off the shower and stepped out, reaching for a white fluffy towel on the bath hook outside the door. "I'm Jerry's wife," she said.

Taz stumbled back, feeling as if she were being pummeled over and over right in her stomach.

"What the fuck is this?" yelled someone from behind her. It was Jerry, standing there, looking into the bathroom, seeing Jenn, his eyes blazing.

Taz was still standing there, feeling like an absolute fool. "I thought that was you in the shower," she said. "But here it is. I'm the person who shouldn't be here."

What she saw in his expression was something she didn't want to analyze too closely—anger, outrage, what? It didn't matter. He had a wife, she was here, and she had access. So who was the fool?

"Of course you should be here," he said. "Why are you here, Jenn?"

Taz was humiliated and needed to put some distance between herself and this situation.

"Jerry, I love you," Jenn said. "I told you that. I brought you a present and planned on showing it to you…"

She didn't want to hear any more as she slipped past him to the bedroom, where she pulled open a drawer and slipped on underwear and another bra. She pulled out a T-shirt without looking too closely and yanked it on along with a pair of jeans.

"Taz, this isn't how it looks." Jerry was there, running his hand over his hair. "I just got here and didn't know she was here," he said. He had that same look on his face as he had before, one that had her thinking he was above board, a truth teller, yet here was a woman saying she was his wife, in his shower, naked.

"Honestly, Jerry, I don't think I want to know. She said she's your wife, present tense, and she's in your shower. Were you maybe coming home to have some fun and have her out the door, or were you expecting me to watch?" Her face burned as she said it along with a nausea in her stomach that had her swallowing and feeling dirty and unwanted. What had she done?

"Of course not. You really think I would bring another woman here and mess around with her with you living here? You really don't think much of me."

"That's not fair, Jerry. I'm not a fool…" She stopped talking as Jenn moved into the bedroom and behind Jerry, not shyly, a towel still wrapped around her amazing figure. She was beautiful and was in their bedroom—correction, his bedroom, with his bed that he'd shared with her. Everything in here, the colors, the comforter, the furnishings, was all her. Taz could see it, and of course she couldn't help feeling as if she were the one who was the other woman. It was screwed up, especially feeling as if she'd walked into something she wanted no part of.

"We're divorced," Jerry said, "and I didn't lie." He took a step toward her as she watched his wife settle on the bed, crossing her long slender legs as if she belonged there. It was too much.

"You know what? Maybe so, but this is not okay. First you never told me about her, and then when you did, you seemed so much like a man who'd been caught cheating, and now this. I'm sorry, but I can't do this. I won't do this. Whatever is going on here, I want no part of it. You said you would have no contact, but here she is…"

Jenn was leaning seductively, staring over at her guy and not saying a word, and Taz could feel something vibrating between them.

"You know what? I'm going to go," Taz said. "You work this out." And then she'd…what? She didn't have a clue. She did, though, need a moment and space and time to figure this out.

She went to step around Jerry, but he reached out to touch her arm. Her eyes went right there, and she just stared at those hands that had brought her so much pleasure but now were crushing her spirit. How could she have misread all of this? She really was a fool. Her throat ached, and she could feel tears burn her eyes, wanting to fall, but she wouldn't give either the satisfaction.

Jerry dropped his hand, and she didn't look up at him as she moved to the doorway. Then, ever so slowly, she glanced back to the first man she'd ever loved. She turned and kept walking.

Chapter 30

"Why are you here?" Jerry said. "Are you trying to make sure I stay miserable forever? And how did you get in?" He leaned against the dresser, taking in Jenn. Beads of water were dripping down over her shoulder, and she dried the ends of her hair with the edge of her towel.

"I wanted to see you," she said. She had a way of sounding contrite that at times left him wanting to wring her neck. So childlike, so innocent, unable to accept responsibility for her actions. And the girl he loved was where? Downstairs. He felt like absolute crap.

"So you snuck in here, how?"

There was a hint of a blush. "I don't want to get him in trouble," she said, pulling in her bottom lip, looking up as if she were so innocent. The blue of her eyes did nothing for him, and he curled his fingers around the edge of the dresser, ready to fire whoever it was.

"Tell me now who it was, Jenn," he demanded.

She took a breath, looking up. "Ben, from your security team. It's not his fault, though. I told him I had a gift for you, and I did. It's downstairs. It's from a new painter, very good. I saw it and thought of you. I showed Ben, and…"

He knew where this was going. "You, what, batted your eyelashes, flashed cleavage, and hinted at sexual possibilities so Ben would give you the key, and you promised you'd bring it right back?" He was tempted to fire Ben, but he knew everyone was aware Jenn was his ex.

"I kind of told him you and I were getting back together." She appeared sheepish for a moment, and maybe it was his expression that had her sitting straighter, her eyes wide. "I'm sorry, I just wanted to see you. I love you, and I made a mistake. Maybe I wanted a chance to win you back. You've always been there for me. We were so good together, and I knew I could get you to see it if I came here."

He gestured around the room. "And what about Taz, my girl? To hell with her? You knew I was involved. I told you she lives here with me. What do you think that's doing to her right now, seeing you naked in my shower? I can't imagine what's going through her head. I just hope she can get past it. I know I'd kill a man who did that to Taz, and I have to wonder whether I'd forgive her. I meant it, Jenn, when I said we were done. I'm changing the locks again. I'll make sure everyone knows you're not allowed in. I need you to respect that, and I need you to stop this. You don't love me. You're just scared because I made everything easier for you, but you were drowning when we were married. You didn't want to be in Denver, and you and I don't want the same things. I want a wife who's here, not traipsing around the globe, someone faithful."

He watched her flush again. Oh, yeah. He'd called it, all right.

"I could be her, that woman you want," she said. She

looked up and slid off the bed, then moved closer to him, her hands up, ready to touch him.

He lifted his arms and moved away. "No, Jenn. This stops. Get dressed, get out. Don't come back." He started to the doorway, looking back at her. "So how many were there?"

She frowned when she looked over to him. "Excuse me?"

"When we were married. I wondered if you cheated. I have my answer, I shouldn't want to know, but I'm asking."

"One, just one," she said, "but it meant nothing. You're the only one who did, and I messed it up. I was scared, is all. I swear I didn't mean for it to ever happen, and I realize now this may be a little late, but I wish I could go back and do everything differently. If you gave me one more chance, I know we could be amazing."

She actually took a step toward him again, and he could see the hope in her eyes as if she believed she could have him back, could make it happen. At the same time, he realized that if he didn't shut it down and kill all the hope she had, there would always be something else and some other way she'd come at him, and then any hope he had of a life with Taz would be over. He couldn't have that. He didn't want that.

"Let me be really clear, Jenn. We're over. Do not call, do not come here. Any help you need, you call someone else. I'll block you so you can't call. I'll call the police if you show up here again. Next is a restraining order." He knew he was being cruel and could see the hurt in her expression. The moment she stepped back, the light dimmed in her eyes and was replaced by a coldness he'd seen a time or two. "Now go get your clothes on and leave," he said.

He didn't wait for her to say another thing, just stepped out into the hallway, went down the stairs, and stood there for a minute, taking in the quiet and nothing else. He looked for Taz in the living room, the kitchen, the dining room, down in his office, and even the laundry room, but she wasn't there. As he walked out, he spotted Jenn hurrying down the stairs in spikes and a dark pantsuit, her hair hastily brushed. She stopped at the bottom. For a moment, he thought she was about to walk to him, but then obviously she thought differently.

"Can I say goodbye?" she said, then gestured to a large frame wrapped in brown paper. It had to be more art. "Your gift. I saw it and thought it was perfect." Then she went to the door and pulled it open, giving him one last look before walking through it and shutting it behind her.

He let out a breath filled with anxiety and worry and everything else that had sucker punched him the moment he'd walked in, heard the voices, and spotted the scene in his bathroom. What could he do to fix this?

"Taz?" he called out but heard nothing, then saw paper on the table against which the framed artwork was leaning. He walked over to it, took in the lined paper and neat penmanship. It was a handwritten note, something he didn't see often.

Jerry, I've gone home. —Taz.

She'd left all her things. He shut his eyes, because this was the one thing he'd never wanted to happen. He needed to talk to her, to show her what she meant, but at the same time he realized she came from a family who wouldn't understand, and her father would likely kill him when he found out what had happened. He had two choices: Let her go, or face the end of a shotgun and do everything he needed to get his girl back.

Chapter 31

It was after midnight when she pulled in front of her cottage and killed her lights, but she wasn't quick enough, as she spotted the lights at her parents' house coming on, followed by the porch light as she stepped out of her truck. The screen creaked, and her dad stepped out in pajama pants and a T-shirt. He was the last person she wanted to speak to. She wanted to sneak into her cottage and crawl into bed, pulling the covers over her head and trying to sleep while the ache in her stomach grew bigger, burning deeper.

"Taz?" he called out and stepped down.

She knew she had no choice. She couldn't ignore him, and she started walking, feeling no excitement. "Yeah, it's me, Dad," she said. The tears she'd cried the first hour out of Denver were sneaking up on her again.

She saw his face, his expression, the alarm the moment he could see her. An instant later, he blurred in front of her, as she couldn't stop the tears as she walked into her father's arms.

"Shh, what happened?" His arms were around her, and he was hugging her.

"Robert, who's here?" her mother called out, and her dad had her turned, walking to the house. Then her mother was there, her arm around her. "Taz, are you okay? What happened?"

Taz couldn't talk as she sobbed, choking and fighting to breathe as she sat on the sofa, her face in her hands, sobbing. Her dad was saying something to her mom, but his hand was on her shoulder, her back, and she felt the sofa cushion dip beside her. Her mom handed her a Kleenex, and she wiped her eyes and blew her nose, taking a minute to see the worry and horror in their expressions. She knew they were thinking something pretty bad.

"I just left," she choked out, her throat closing up before she could say anything else.

She saw the exchange between them, and then her dad got up and left the room. Her mom moved beside her on the sofa, sliding her arm around her shoulder. "Did Jerry do something? I don't understand. You just drove away? You should have called us."

Then her dad was back and perched on the sofa table in front of her. He was so close, and she saw his worry. She shrugged, because the problem was that she hadn't thought much after scribbling that note and getting in her truck. She just needed to be home, here, where she was safe and wouldn't feel as if she were drowning.

"I made a mistake going with Jerry. I knew it was too good to be true. He was married." The moment she said it, she saw the crossness in her father's brow. "He's divorced, I mean. He was married. I just… There was so much about him I didn't know."

Her parents exchanged another glance, and then her

dad said, "Taz, why don't you start at the beginning and tell us what happened?"

How to explain what she'd walked in on, seeing his ex naked in his shower when she'd thought it was Jerry himself and she'd planned to join him for some hot shower sex? She was struggling on how to censor it, but she saw the moment they understood as she stumbled through the scene.

"Susan, why don't you make our girl some soup?" her dad said, and her mom rubbed her arm and stepped around them in her nightgown, her flower housecoat overtop.

"You probably think I'm a fool," Taz said.

Her dad said nothing as he just looked at her and then glanced away, thinking something—what, she wasn't sure. Then he shook his head. "I don't know what to say, Taz. I didn't expect that from Jerry. You say his ex was in the shower but Jerry wasn't there. He came in after. Did he plan for her to be there, or what?"

"Well, no. I think he was as surprised as me, but she loves him and said as much, and—"

"And has he acted inappropriately? Was he seeing her too? I guess I'm trying to find out whether there's any merit to that idea, or was she sneaking in, trying to set the stage to destroy your relationship?"

She didn't have a clue what to say to that. She tried to explain, tried to get her tongue to move, but her dad shook his head as if she didn't get it.

"You forget, Taz, I have six daughters. You're good girls, but I also know that although men can be assholes, women can be vicious, too, especially when it comes to men they've set their sights on. You'd do well to think about that. He should have told you he was married before, and absolutely so if his ex-wife is still in the picture, but be sure you know everything and have the right story before you do something you could regret, is all I'm saying." He had his hands clasped when her mom walked back in with a tray of steaming chicken soup and a glass of milk and set it on the table beside her dad.

Then her dad stood up and had another exchange with her mom. It was just a look, but something that passed between them gave away their years of closeness and understanding. They each knew what the other was thinking. "In the morning, Taz, whatever you decide, you know we'll stick by you. This is your home always. Just make sure you're not running and hiding because you don't want to face the situation and talk. A relationship is work, not easy. You need to share and talk, but it's also better to know early if it won't work."

"Eat your soup, drink your milk, and then get some sleep," her mom added, and for the first time, Taz felt as if she could just be, just sleep and not have to worry about anything else that night.

SHE WAS in bed still and heard voices outside as the sun filled her cabin. She'd borrowed a nightgown from her mom, as she'd left with only the clothes on her back. She heard footsteps, and then her door opened.

"Taz, you asleep still?" It was Naomi.

She heard Ivy say something, too, and then more footsteps.

"Didn't she answer?" That was Mason.

Taz pulled the duvet over her head when she heard Scarlett's voice. Their footsteps were approaching the loft, and then one of them bounced on the bed, then another.

"Get off me!" she said, pulling the covers back to see Scarlett and Mason on the bed. Ivy was leaning over her and rested her hand on her forehead. Naomi's dark hair was pulled back in a ponytail, her glasses on, and she was staring at her as if trying to figure out what had happened.

"What did he do?" Ivy said, reaching for her wrist and taking her pulse.

Taz pulled her arm away. "I'm not sick, and if you don't mind, y'all, I'm tired. I want to sleep, so leave, please."

"Oh, I think not. Did he hurt you, hit you, throw you out?" Naomi stepped closer, and Taz took in the eyes of all her sisters waiting for her to enlighten them. Then she heard a car. Every one of them raced to the window. Mason jumped off the bed, but not before Scarlett.

"Oh my good God," Scarlett said. "He's here."

"Who's here?" Taz asked as her sisters all gave her a look of total shock.

"Jerry, and he's talking with Daddy," Mason said. "Come on, this is too good. You have to tell us."

"I don't have to tell you," Taz said. "Are you sure it's him?" She climbed out of bed and looked out her bedroom window, seeing Jerry. Whatever he was saying to her father, he seemed upset and wasn't about to leave. She moved back from the window when they both looked over as if they knew she was watching them. She couldn't help feeling as if she'd been caught doing something she shouldn't have. Her dad said something, and Jerry started walking toward her cabin. She couldn't believe her dad wasn't stopping him. She backed away and over to the stairs, fighting her panic.

"Is he really coming over here?" she heard Scarlett say.

Taz moved to the stairs, grabbing her clothes off the floor. She was halfway down when the door opened and he spotted her. Everything in his look, his gaze, pinned her right there. She was bumped from behind by one of her sisters—which one, she didn't know, because she didn't look back.

She didn't say a thing as she stared at him, and then slowly she realized he was taking in all of them.

"You know what?" Ivy said. "Why don't we all give you some privacy? Scarlett, Mason, Naomi, come on. Let's let these two talk and work this out." Ivy herded her sisters down and gave one last look to Taz before stopping in front of Jerry, looking up to him, and saying. "You hurt her, and we'll kill you and stuff your body somewhere it'll never be found." Then she patted his chest once before glancing back to Taz again. "Call us if you need us," she said, then stepped out after her sisters and pulled the door closed.

"You left with just a note," Jerry said, his arms crossed. He didn't move.

She started down the stairs on shaky legs until she was at the bottom, holding day-old clothes, wearing her mother's knee-length white nightgown. "I did. I…your ex was in your shower as if she had every right to be there. I can't…" She was shaking her head, and he walked toward her.

"You have every right to be outraged, upset, angry, hurt, all of that, but running out on me, on us, wasn't okay," he said. "I didn't know she was there. I told you before that we were done. She talked an employee of mine into giving her a key, and she snuck in. It was a ploy, and it won't happen again." He was about five feet from her, and she didn't want to move any closer as she tried to figure out what to think, what to do.

"I don't like her," Taz said. "She wants you back, and she won't stop until she has you."

"You're wrong, Taz. She will stop. I made sure she knows she went too far this time. But so did you."

That made no sense. She wasn't the one in the wrong.

"How do you think I felt, seeing your note, knowing that instead of sticking around, you didn't trust me enough to talk to me? Instead you bolted, and here I was worrying about you. Your dad called late last night."

She didn't know what to say. She glanced to the window, wondering why her dad would do something like that.

"No matter what happened, he was right to do it," Jerry said. "I like your dad. You ran out, Taz. There's nothing between Jenn and me. She can't get in again, and she knows if there's ever a next time, I'll call the police and get a restraining order.

She couldn't believe he'd said that. Now she felt like absolute crap. "I'm sorry. I don't know what to say."

He took another step toward her, and this time he held out his hand. She just looked at it as he waited, then slowly reached out, taking a step forward and setting her hand in his. He pulled her in the rest of the way, sliding his other hand around her waist, her hips. "Jenn and I could never work because she was too busy running for everything else," he said. "I want a wife who's there, who wants to make a relationship work, to be there, to talk and share everything with me. I need to know, if the going gets tough again, are you going to run?"

He'd said "wife." She heard it and couldn't get her tongue to move.

She shook her head and swallowed. "No," she said, "but I won't share you."

Then he pulled his hand away, reaching into his pocket. He pulled out a small box and held it out. Taz took it, her hand shaking as she opened it and saw a pear-shaped diamond set in white gold. She flicked her gaze to him when he said, "I won't share you, either. Marry me."

She took in the ring again and lifted her hand as he pulled it from the box. "Yes," she said, and he slipped it on her finger, and she allowed him to pull her close and kiss her deeply.

Turn the page for a sneak peek of
*THE DATING GAME the next book in THE PARKER
SISTERS*
Available in eBook, Audio and Paperback

From a Readers' Favorite award—winning author and "queen of the family saga" (Aherman) comes The Parker Sisters a new spinoff series of the Married in Montana series.

Twenty Six year old Ivy Parker is a Nurse by day, but an unlikely attraction with a mysterious man will turn her world upside down as she finds herself in, The Dating Game.

CHAPTER 1

"**D**amn, she looks beautiful," said twenty-six-year-old Ivy Parker. She couldn't keep her eyes from the scene in front of her: her sister Taz on the makeshift dance floor in the arms of her husband of five hours, Jerry O'Rourke—and man, could he dance.

Taz's white gown swept the floor, cut low in the back and front, and her dark hair was pinned up with orchids. Jerry was dashing in his elegant black tux, and for the first time it hit Ivy how right they looked together. It was a happy thought that left her feeling so sad and lonely.

"Happy too, the bitch," said Naomi, her sister, who was also a bridesmaid and very much as single as Ivy. The two stood in identical peach gowns that draped to their ankles. The only problem was that the dress looked better on all her sisters' slender frames, whereas it seemed to add at least twenty pounds to Ivy's size ten—okay, maybe twelve if she was being honest. She'd finally stopped looking in the mirror, horrified at how the dress looked like a grain sack on her and made her ass look far bigger than she knew it was. Another reason, she was sure, that she was fighting to keep a smile pasted to her face.

"What are you two going on about?" said Brandyne, their eldest sister, as she slipped in between them and put her arms around them. Her dark hair was long and wavy to her slim waist, and her wedding ring was the first thing Ivy had noticed of late. Brandyne was married to a Montana sheriff, with five kids from a cowboy she'd hooked up with years before. She too was slender and curvy. Damn, so unfair.

"Oh, you know, our sister over there dancing with Jerry. Still can't believe she's married, and so soon after meeting the guy. She traded us all in and left us, just like you," Ivy said. She glanced over her shoulder to Brandyne, who seemed a little startled. Naomi too gave her an odd look. She shrugged. "Sorry, just things are changing faster than…" She stopped talking when Brandyne and Naomi's disapproving glares turned darker.

"Boy, are you ever in a funk," Brandyne said, and Naomi nodded in agreement. "Shake it off. This is Taz's day. I hope to all hell you didn't lay any of this at her feet?"

"No, of course not. I smiled and did everything I was supposed to as the maid of honor: fussed over her, did her nails, got her some sexy underwear with garters and an indecent lacy push-up bra. Jerry's going to go weak at the knees when he pulls her dress off tonight. I even provided the necessary shot of whiskey when Daddy showed up to lead her down the aisle and I saw the panic about to take hold at what she'd gotten herself into."

Her sisters were still looking at her oddly. She decided it was best to leave out the part where she'd offered to drive the getaway car just in case the last-minute jitters and panic attack were Taz's intuition's way of stepping up to warn her about the giant mistake she was about to make.

No, she figured that part would likely get her a scolding from just about everyone, considering even Taz had burst into laughter, believing the offer was Ivy's sense of humor gone wild. It wasn't, but Ivy noted painfully that it had been the confidence boost her sister needed to get up, take her father's arm, and practically skip down the aisle to say "I do."

Scarlett, their seventeen-year-old sister, bounced to Ivy's other side. She was in a party mood. "OMG, have you seen all the hot guys Jerry invited? I swear this is the most fun I've ever had and the best party this county has ever seen." Her short dark hair was growing out but still made her round cheeks and bold, mischievous eyes really pop. Then she set her hand over her heart in such a dramatic way. "I still can't believe she's married and living in Denver, and there's now, what, four of us left? Wonder what Daddy and Mama will do with Taz's cottage?"

From her expression, Ivy could see the calculations going on in Scarlett's mind. She was over-the-top dramatic about everything and was always looking for the angle, for what was best for her.

"Do you think Daddy will let me have it?" she said. There it was, all about her.

"Yeah, don't think so, Scarlett," Ivy said as she took in all the guests, three hundred neighbors, friends, and distant cousins along with a few of Jerry's family and business associates—hence the drop-dead gorgeous guys with hot babes on their arms. Her parents were also now on the dance floor. Riske, the live band Jerry had brought in, were clients of his and were currently at the top of the charts, another reason Scarlett was beside herself. They were good and loud.

"You know what, Ivy? Your turn will come," Brandyne said. "You'll find your Mr. Right, your perfect partner, and then you'll be the one up there looking so happy and over the moon."

Ivy couldn't even pretend to believe a word she was saying, so she just grunted. Unlike Scarlett, Ivy hated being the center of attention and anyone making a fuss over her.

"Looks like Mama's having a great time," Brandyne said. "Haven't seen her laugh like that in a long while."

Her dad was a pretty good dancer, too, and her mom glowed in her cream dress, smiling and relaxed for the first time since the wedding plans had begun.

"You're right," Ivy said. "She was a wreck, worried and nervous right up until they said 'I do.' She's the wedding coordinator, the one who made this dog and pony show, as Daddy's put it several times over the past few weeks, a reality." She gestured to the magnificent huge tent that had arrived on a flatbed along with all of the tables and kitchen equipment the caterers needed at their disposal.

"This is awesome," Scarlett said. "Exactly how I want my wedding, lavish, expensive, all the flowers, the crystal, the meal served by waiters—but I'd also like ice sculptures and champagne, and white doves released just when we say 'I do.'" She pressed her hand to her chest, and Ivy was absolutely speechless. Apparently so were Naomi and Brandyne, who exchanged a look as if Scarlett had lost her mind.

"So anyone know where they're off to on their honeymoon?" Ivy said. She hadn't a clue, and Taz had said it was a surprise. Jerry wouldn't even tell her whether she needed a bikini or a parka, just that they'd be flying off after the reception tonight and he'd taken care of packing her things.

"Can I have your attention, please?" the emcee said. "I need all the single women up here on the dance floor. The bride is going to be throwing the bouquet. All you single guys, don't worry. Your turn's coming up next."

A hand wrapped around her wrist. "Come on, Ivy." It was Mason, their youngest sister, her hair dyed strawberry red to match the dress, she said, though Ivy thought it clashed with the peach.

Mason pulled her into the already crowded dance floor, which was packed with all the single women of Kaycee. Ivy slipped to the back, hoping to hide and make her way out of the tent into the dark. She peeked around Martha, the town's thin and reedy librarian, who had thick glasses and an overbite, to see the closest opening. Everyone was counting, and she was being shoved by Tina, the drugstore clerk, thirty and single, who was literally fisting her hands and flexing her muscles, obviously prepared to take down anyone who got between her and that bouquet. Tina shouted something, pumping her fist in the air, which had Ivy taking a step to the side and squeezing through the women pushing behind her.

She was shoved and then bumped, her foot stepped on as she slinked to the edge of the tent. She could see Brandyne and her handsome sheriff husband, Blake, laughing at the sidelines, most likely at the crazed women all determined to be the one to catch that bouquet, as if it were any guarantee that person would actually be next to marry. What a stupid tradition! Ivy wanted no part of it.

"Two!" she heard the emcee shout from the stage.

The women were all screaming, and she was one step closer to freedom and sanity. She lifted her dress as her feet pinched in the ridiculously high sandals she'd squeezed them into. The women were going nuts. She was elbowed from behind and grabbed a chair when she nearly lost her balance. "Excuse me, sorry about that," she muttered to who she thought was Irene, the owner of the local bar, in her late forties.

"One!"

She stepped to the edge of the tent.

"Ivy Parker, would you stand still so I can throw these flowers your way? Get on back here," Taz yelled out, and everyone turned to face her where she stood, one high-heeled foot on the dirt outside the tent and one on the makeshift floor that would be gone the next day. She wanted to kill her sister as she gestured to cut it out.

Too late. Everyone was looking her way as the flowers flew in a near perfect line drive and hit her in the face. She grabbed them only to preserve her dignity as she stumbled back. She was sure her heels would break, her ankle twisting. Warm large hands gripped her waist.

"Whoa, there," the man said. He had a deep voice and was tall, dark haired, and totally ripped, from what she could tell in the navy suit he wore. His tie was loosened, and he was strong, judging by the way he lifted her as if she weighed nothing and set her back on her feet.

"Yeah…" She couldn't think of what else to say, holding a bouquet, hearing her sisters in the background and ignoring every one of them. She felt stupid. He was rough and gorgeous, not pretty but hard, chiseled, now smiling at her as if teasing her.

He glanced over her head and let his hand fall from her waist. "Think you're being summoned." He gestured with his chin.

"Ivy, get on back here!" Taz said, now holding the mic. Ivy wanted to kick her as she shook her head, intent on getting the hell out of there. She was done with this spec-tacle and refused to be dragged to the center of the floor to be displayed as a spinster, to have it pointed out to everyone that hey, just maybe she was next, as if being single were something to be ashamed of.

"I think they want you back there," he said. She was sure now she could hear the laughter in his voice.

"Yeah, no, I think not," she said and laughed, then nearly cringed at the giddy sound in her voice. She didn't do giddy. What the hell?

He was still smiling, and the light touched his amber eyes. He had long lashes for a guy. Who'd have thought they would make him that much hotter? She was envious. Then a hand gripped her arm and she was yanked away.

"Scarlett, let go of me," she said and batted at her. Scarlett was unbelievably strong. Flower petals fell to the floor around them.

"Since you just had to catch the bouquet, you know the tradition. You're now next to get married. So you just stand here like a good girl and wait for the guys' turn."

Ivy could hear the jealousy spitting from her sister and wanted to correct her about all of it. "You know what? You take it. It's all yours. I'll just get on out of here." She tried to hand the flowers over, but Scarlett gave her the flat of her hand.

"Too late," she said and left Ivy to stand like an idiot, alone on the dance floor.

The few guys who stepped up cheered and hollered as Taz lifted her leg on a stool and Jerry lifted her skirt, showing her bare leg and the garter on her thigh. He slipped it off her leg, balled it in his fist, and tossed it. The five men there all jumped, and time stood still.

A hand in the air held the garter, and the men parted to reveal the brown tweed and pot belly of Vern Butterfield, the seventy-year-old widower from the next spread over.

"Good God," she heard Naomi hiss from behind her.

Then she was pushed to the center of the floor as Vern made the face of a man who'd had too much to drink and had just won the lottery as he strutted toward her. The band started up, and he grabbed her hand.

"Hey, my lucky night," he said. "Guess this dance is mine." He stank of one too many beers as he rested a sweaty hand on the small of her back, whipping her around as if he could dance, which he couldn't. He just jumped with two left feet.

All she could think was that this was about as bad as it could get.

About the Author

"Lorhainne Eckhart is one of my go to authors when I want a guaranteed good book. So many twists and turns, but also so much love and such a strong sense of family."

(Lora W., Reviewer)

New York Times & USA Today bestseller Lorhainne Eckhart is best known for her writing Raw Relatable Real Romances, where "Morals and family are running themes. Danger, romance, and a drive to do what is right will see you glued to the page." As one fan calls her, she is the "Queen of the family saga." (aherman) writing "the ups and downs of what goes on within a family but also with some suspense, angst and of course a bit of romance thrown in for good measure." Follow Lorhainne on Bookbub to receive alerts on New Releases and Sales and join her mailing list at LorhainneEckhart.com for her Monday Blog, books news, giveaways and FREE reads. With over 120 books, audiobooks, and multiple series published and available at all retailers now translated into six languages. She is a multiple recipient of the Readers' Favorite Award for Suspense and Romance, and lives in the Pacific Northwest on an island, is the mother of three, her oldest has autism and she is an advocate for never giving up on your dreams.

"Lorhainne Eckhart has this uncanny way of just hitting the spot every time with her books."

(Caroline L., Reviewer)

The O'Connells: *The O'Connells of Livingston, Montana are not your typical family. A riveting collection of stories surrounding the ups and downs of what goes on within a family but also with some suspense, angst and of course a bit of romance thrown in for good measure "I thought I loved the Friessens, but I absolutely adore the O'Connell's. Each and every book has totally different genres of stories but the one thing in common is how she is able to wrap it around the family which is the heart of each story." (C. Logue)*

The Friessens: *An emotional big family romance series, the Friessen family siblings find their relationships tested, lay their hearts on the line, and discover lasting love! "Lorhainne Eckhart is one of my go to authors when I want a guaranteed good book. So many twists and turns, but also so much love and such a strong sense of family." (Lora W., Reviewer)*

The Parker Sisters: *The Parker Sisters are a close-knit family, and like any other family they have their ups and downs. "Eckhart has crafted another intense family drama…The character development is outstanding, and the emotional investment is high…" (Aherman, Reviewer)*

The McCabe Brothers: *Join the five McCabe siblings on their journeys to the dark and dangerous side of love! An intense, exhilarating collection of romantic thrillers you won't want to miss. — "Eckhart has a new series that is definitely worth the read. The queen of the family saga started this series with a spin-off of her wildly successful Friessen series." From a Readers' Favorite award—winning author and "queen of the family saga" (Aherman)*

Billy Jo McCabe Mystery: *The social worker and the cop, an unlikely couple drawn together on a small, secluded Pacific Northwest island where nothing is as it seems. Protecting the innocent comes at a cost, and what seems to be a sleepy, quiet town is anything but.*

Lorhainne loves to hear from her readers! You can connect with me at:
www.LorhainneEckhart.com
lorhainneeckhart.le@gmail.com

facebook.com/AuthorLorhainneEckhart

twitter.com/LEckhart

instagram.com/lorhainneeckhart

bookbub.com/profile/lorhainne-eckhart

pinterest.com/lorhainneeckhart

In the Family
In the Silence
In the Charm
Unexpected Consequences
It Was Always You
The First Time I Saw You
Welcome to My Arms
Welcome to Boston
I'll Always Love You
Ground Rules
A Reason to Breathe
You Are My Everything
Anything For You
The Homecoming
Stay Away From My Daughter
The Bad Boy
A Place of Our Own
The Visitor
All About Devon
Long Past Dawn
How to Heal a Heart
Keep Me In Your Heart

The O'Connells

The Neighbor
The Third Call
The Secret Husband
The Quiet Day
The Commitment
The Missing Father
The Hometown Hero
Justice
The Family Secret

The Fallen O'Connell
The Return of the O'Connells
And The She Was Gone
The Stalker
The O'Connell Family Christmas
The Girl Next Door

The McCabe Brothers
Don't Stop Me (Vic)
Don't Catch Me (Chase)
Don't Run From Me (Aaron)
Don't Hide From Me (Luc)
Don't Leave Me (Claudia)
Out of Time

A Billy Jo McCabe Mystery
Nothing As it Seems
Hiding in Plain Sight
The Cold Case
The Trap
Above the Law

The Wilde Brothers
The One (Joe and Margaret)
The Honeymoon, A Wilde Brothers Short
Friendly Fire (Logan and Julia)
Not Quite Married, A Wilde Brothers Short
A Matter of Trust (Ben and Carrie)
The Reckoning, A Wilde Brothers Christmas
Traded (Jake)
Unforgiven (Samuel)
The Holiday Bride

Married in Montana
His Promise
Love's Promise
A Promise of Forever

The Parker Sisters
Thrill of the Chase
The Dating Game
Play Hard to Get
What We Can't Have
Go Your Own Way
A June Wedding

Kate & Walker
One Night
Edge of Night
Last Night

Walk the Right Road Series
The Choice
Lost and Found
Merkaba
Bounty
Blown Away: The Final Chapter

The Saved Series
Saved
Vanished
Captured

Single Titles
He Came Back
Loving Christine

For my German Readers
Die Außenseiter-Reihe
Der Vergessene Junge
Der Gefallene Held

For my French Readers
L'ENFANT OUBLIÉ

www.ingramcontent.com/pod-product-compliance
Lightning Source LLC
Chambersburg PA
CBHW030942210726
48290CB00007B/2297